Romeo's grip tightened and one finger caught her chin and raised her face to his spear-sharp gaze. Her stomach knotted at the savage determination on his face.

'They will never get their hands on you or our son. You have my word on this, Maisie.'

She shook her head, her insides growing colder by the second. 'But you can't guarantee that, can you? Or you wouldn't be here with six bodyguards in tow.'

'There's one way to ensure your safety,' he said, his gaze raking her face as if he wanted to pull the answer from her even before he'd asked the question.

'What's that?' she murmured.

'You will marry me. Then you and our son will know the protection of my name.'

Secret Heirs of Billionaires

There are some things money can't buy...

Living life at lightning pace, these magnates are no strangers to stakes at their highest. It seems they've got it all… That is until they find out that there's an unplanned item to add to their list of accomplishments!

Achieved:

1. Successful business empire

2. Beautiful women in their bed

3. *An heir to bear their name...?*

Though every billionaire needs to leave his legacy in safe hands, discovering a secret heir shakes up his carefully orchestrated plan in more ways than one!

Uncover their secrets in:

Unwrapping the Castelli Secret by Caitlin Crews
Brunetti's Secret Son by Maya Blake

Look out for more stories in
The Secret Heirs of Billionaires series in 2016!

millsandboon.co.uk

BRUNETTI'S
SECRET SON

BY
MAYA BLAKE

First published in Great Britain 2015
by Mills & Boon, an imprint of Harlequin (UK) Limited,
Eton House, 18-24 Paradise Road, Richmond, Surrey, TW9 1SR

© 2015 Maya Blake

ISBN: 978-0-263-26051-9

Maya Blake's hopes of becoming a writer were born when she picked up her first romance aged thirteen. Little did she know her dream would come true! Does she still pinch herself every now and then, to make sure it's not a dream? Yes, she does!

Feel free to pinch her too, via Twitter, Facebook or Goodreads! Happy reading!

Books by Maya Blake

Mills & Boon Modern Romance

Married for the Prince's Convenience
Innocent in His Diamonds
His Ultimate Prize
Marriage Made of Secrets
The Sinful Art of Revenge
The Price of Success

The Untameable Greeks

What the Greek's Money Can't Buy
What the Greek Can't Resist
What the Greek Wants Most

The 21st Century Gentleman's Club

The Ultimate Playboy

Visit the Author Profile page
at millsandboon.co.uk for more titles.

CHAPTER ONE

THE HIDEOUS MANSION was just as he'd recalled in his nightmares, the gaudy orange exterior clashing wildly with the massive blue shutters. The only thing that didn't quite gel with the picture before him was the blaze of the sun glinting off the grotesquely opulent marble statues guarding the entry gates.

Romeo Brunetti's last memory of this place had been in the chilling rain, his threadbare clothes sticking to his skin as he'd huddled in the bushes outside the gates. A part of him had prayed he wouldn't be discovered, the other more than a tiny bit hopeful that discovery would mean the end to all the suffering, the hunger, the harrowing pain of rejection that ate his thirteen-year-old body alive from morning to night. Back then he would've welcomed the beating his reluctant rescuer had received for daring to return Romeo to this place. Because the beating would have ended in oblivion, and the bitterness coursing through his veins like acid would have been no more.

Unfortunately, the fates had decreed otherwise. He'd hidden in the bushes, cold and near catatonic, until the ever-present hunger had forced him to move.

Romeo stared up at the spears clutched in the hands of the statues, recalling his father's loud-bellied boast of them being made of solid gold.

The man who'd called him a bastard and a waste of space to his face. Right before he'd instructed his minion to throw him out and make sure he never returned. That he didn't care whether the spawn of the whore he'd rutted with in an alleyway in Palermo lived or died, as long as he, Agostino

Fattore, the head of the ruling crime family, didn't have to see the boy's face again.

No…not his *father*.

The man didn't deserve that title.

Romeo's hands tightened on the steering wheel of his Ferrari and he wondered for the thousandth time why he'd bothered to come to this place. Why he'd let a letter he'd shredded in a fit of cold rage seconds after reading it compel him into going back on the oath he'd made to himself over two decades ago. He looked over to the right where the towering outer wall to the late Agostino Fattore's estate rose into the sky, and sure enough, the bush was exactly as he remembered it, its leafy branches spread out, offering the same false sanctuary.

For a wild moment, Romeo fought the strong urge to lunge out of the car and rip the bush out of the earth with his bare hands, tear every leaf and branch to shreds. Tightening his jaw, he finally lowered his window and punched in the code his memory had cynically retained.

As the gates creaked open, he questioned again why he was doing this. So what if the letter had hinted at something else? What could the man whose rejection had been brutally cold and complete have to offer him in death that he'd failed so abjectly to offer in life?

Because he needed answers.

He needed to know that the blood running through his veins didn't have an unknown stranglehold over him that would turn his life upside down when he least expected it.

That the two times in his life when he'd lost control to the point of not recognising himself would be the only times he would feel savagely unmoored.

No one but Romeo knew how much he regretted wasting the four years of his life after the bitter night he'd been here last, looking for acceptance anywhere and any way he could find it. More than hating the man whose blood ran through his veins, Romeo hated the years he'd spent trying to find a replacement for Agostino Fattore.

Giving himself permission to close his heart off at seventeen had been the best decision he'd ever made.

So why are you here? You're nothing like him.

He needed to be sure. Agostino might no longer be alive, but he needed to look into the heart of Fattore's legacy and reassure himself that the lost little boy who'd thought his world would end because of another's rejection was obliterated completely.

Impatient with himself for prevaricating, Romeo smashed his foot on the accelerator and grunted in satisfaction as the tyres squealed on the asphalt road leading to the courtyard. Unfolding himself from the driver's seat, he stalked up to the iron-studded double doors and slammed them open.

Striding into the chequer-tiled hallway, he glared at the giant antique chandelier above his head. If he had cared whether this house stood or fell, that monstrosity would have been the first thing in the incinerator. But he wasn't here to ponder the ugly tastes of a dead man. He was here to finally slay ghosts.

Ghosts that had lingered at the back of his consciousness since he was a child but that had been resurrected one night five years ago, in the arms of a woman who'd made him lose control.

He turned as slow feet shuffled in his direction, followed by firmer footholds that drew a grim smile from Romeo. So, the old order hadn't changed. Or maybe the strength of Romeo's anger had somehow transmitted to Fattore's former second in command, prompting the old man who approached to seek the protection of his bodyguards.

Lorenzo Carmine threw out his hands in greeting, but Romeo glimpsed the wariness in the old man's eyes. 'Welcome, *mio figlio*. Come, I have lunch waiting for us.'

Romeo tensed. 'I'm not your son and this meeting will not last beyond five minutes, so I suggest you tell me what

you withheld in your letter right now and stop wasting my
time.' He didn't bother to hide the sneer in his voice.

Lorenzo's pale grey eyes flared with a temper Romeo
had witnessed the last time he was here. But along with it
came the recognition that Romeo was no longer a fright-
ened little boy incapable of defending himself. Slowly, his
expression altered into a placid smile.

'You have to pardon me. My constitution requires that I
strictly regulate my mealtimes or I suffer for it.'

Romeo turned towards the door, again regretting his decision to come here. He was wasting his time looking for
answers in stone and concrete. He was wasting his time,
full stop.

'Then by all means go and look after your constitution.
Enjoy the rest of your days and don't bother contacting me
again.' He stepped towards the door, a note of relief spiking
through him at the thought of leaving this place.

'Your father left something for you. Something you will
want to see.'

Romeo stopped. 'He was not my father and there's nothing he possesses in this life or the next that could possibly
interest me.'

Lorenzo sighed. 'And yet you came all this way at my
request. Or was it just to stick out your middle finger at an
old man?'

Romeo's jaw clenched, hating that the question he'd been
asking himself fell from the lips of a man who'd spent his
whole life being nothing but a vicious thug. 'Just spit it out,
Carmine,' he gritted out.

Lorenzo glanced at the nearer bodyguard and nodded.
The beefy minder headed down the long hallway and disappeared.

'For the sake of my friend, your father, the Almighty rest
his soul, I will go against my doctor's wishes.' The remaining guard fell into step behind Lorenzo, who indicated a
room to their left.

From memory, Romeo knew it was the holding room for visitors, a garishly decorated antechamber that led to the receiving room, where his father had loved to hold court.

The old man shuffled to a throne-like armchair and sank heavily into it. Romeo chose to remain standing and curbed the need to pace like a caged animal.

Although he'd come through the desolation of his ragged past, he didn't care for the brutal reminders everywhere he looked. The corner of this room was where he'd crouched when his father's loud lambasting of a minion had led to gunshots and horrific screams the first time he'd been brought here. The gilt-framed sofa was where his father had forced him to sit and watch as he'd instructed his lieutenants to beat Paolo Giordano into a pulp.

He didn't especially care for the reminder that it was possibly because of Fattore's blood running through his veins that he'd almost taken the same violent path when, tired of living on the streets, he'd almost joined a terror-loving gang feared for their ruthlessness.

Sì, he should've stayed far away, in the warmth of his newest and most lavish by-invitation-only Caribbean resort.

His eyes narrowed as the second bodyguard returned with a large ornately carved antique box and handed it to Lorenzo. 'It's a good thing your father chose to keep an eye on you, wasn't it?' Lorenzo said.

'Scusi?' Romeo rasped in astonishment.

Lorenzo waved his hand. 'Your mother, the Almighty rest *her* unfortunate soul, attempted to do her best, but we all knew she didn't have what it took, eh?'

Romeo barely stopped his lips from curling. The subject of his mother was one he'd sealed under strict lock and key, then thrown into a vault the night he'd buried her five years ago.

The same night he'd let his guard down spectacularly with a woman whose face continued to haunt him when he least expected it. A woman who had, for the first time in a long time, made him want to feel the warmth of human emotion.

A tremor went through him at the memory, its deep and disturbing effect as potent, if not more so, than it'd been that night when he'd realised that his emotions weren't as clinical and icy as he'd imagined them to be.

He shut down that line of thought.

Maisie O'Connell had had no place in his life then, save as a means of achieving a few hours of oblivion, and she most certainly didn't have one now, in this cursed place. Like the bush outside this miscreation of a mansion, she represented a time in his life he wanted banished for all time.

Because it makes you uncomfortable...vulnerable even? Basta!

'You seem to be under the misapprehension that I'll indulge you in fond trips down potholed memory lanes. Be assured that I will not. If I remember correctly, *you* helped to throw me out of the gates when I was a child. Your exact words, presumably passed down from my father, were—*I see you again, you leave in a body bag.*'

Lorenzo shrugged. 'Those were hot-headed days. Look at you now. You've done very well for yourself despite your less than salubrious beginning.' A touch of malice flared in his eyes. 'None of us imagined a boy conceived in the gutter would rise to such esteem.'

Romeo shoved his hands in his pockets so he wouldn't do the unthinkable and strangle the old man where he sat. 'Then I guess it's a good thing I was intelligent enough to realise early on that whether you were born in the gutter or with a dozen golden spoons clutched in your fist, our lives are what we make them. Otherwise, who knows where I'd be today? In a mental institution, perhaps? Bemoaning my fate while rocking back and forth in a straitjacket?'

The old man laughed, or he attempted to. When the sound veered into a bone-jarring coughing spell, his bodyguards exchanged wary glances before one stepped forward with a glass of water.

Lorenzo's violent refusal of help had the guard springing back into his designated position. When the coughing fit passed, Lorenzo opened the box and took out several papers.

'You were never going to go down without a fight. I saw that in you even when you were a boy. But you'll do well to remember where that intelligence comes from.'

'Are you really suggesting that I owe what I've made of myself to you or the pathetic band of thugs you call a family?' he asked, incredulous.

Lorenzo waved him away. 'We'll discuss what you owe in a bit. Your father meant to do this before he was tragically taken from us,' he muttered.

Romeo curbed the need to voice his suspicions that his father's departure from this life hadn't been tragic at all; that the boat explosion that had taken his life and those of his wife and the two half-sisters Romeo had never been allowed to meet hadn't been accidental, but the target of a carefully orchestrated assassination.

Instead, he watched Lorenzo pull out document after document and lay them on the desk.

'The first order of business is this house. It's yours free and clear from any financial obligations. All the lawyers need is your signature to take possession. It comes with the collection of cars, the horses and the three hundred acres of land, of course.'

Astonishment rendered Romeo speechless.

'Then there are the businesses. They're not doing as well as we'd hoped, and certainly not as well as your own businesses are doing. The Carmelo *famiglia* mistakenly believe this is an excuse for them to start making moves on Fattore business, but I suspect that will all turn around once our business has been brought under the umbrella of your company, Brunetti International—'

Romeo laughed. 'You must be out of your mind if you

think I want any part of this blood-soaked legacy. I'd rather
return to the gutter than claim a single brick of this house,
or associate myself in any way with the Fattore name and
everything it stands for.'

'You may despise the Fattore name, but do you think
Brunetti, son of a two-bit whore has a better ring?' Lorenzo sneered.

It didn't, but in the bleak, terrible hellhole of his childhood it had been the better of two evils. Especially since that
greater evil had warned him never to use the name *Fattore*.

'This is your legacy, no matter how much you try to deny
it,' Lorenzo insisted.

'You can sit there and rewrite history until the walls
crumble around you,' Romeo enunciated with a burning
intensity he suspected would erupt the longer he spent in
this house. 'But your five minutes have come and gone, old
man. And this meeting is well and truly over. Any problems
you have with your extortion business and territorial wars
with the Carmelo family are yours to deal with.'

He made it to the door before Lorenzo spoke.

'Your father suspected that when the time came you
would prove intransigent. So he asked me to give you this.'

For the second time, Romeo froze, his instincts screech-
ing at him to keep walking, but his brain warning that to do
as he so desperately wanted would be unwise.

Lorenzo held out a large manila envelope, which he slid
across the desk with a smug look.

'I told you I'm not interested in anything bearing the Fattore name. Whatever is in that envelope—'

'Is of a more…personal nature and will interest you, *mio
figlio*. I'm confident of it.'

Romeo abandoned the need to remind the old man not
to call him son. Lorenzo was enjoying needling him a little too much, and Romeo was fast reaching boiling point.

Striding across the room, he snatched up the envelope
and ripped it open. The first picture punched him in the

gut, expelling a harsh breath. It showed him standing at his mother's graveside, the only attendee besides the priest, as Ariana Brunetti was laid to rest.

He flung the picture on the desk, his mouth twisting as the next picture showed him in funereal black, sitting at his hotel bar, staring into a glass of cognac.

'So Fattore had me followed for an afternoon five years ago. Perhaps he would've better profited using that time to tend his businesses.'

Lorenzo tented his fingers. 'Keep going. The best is yet to come.'

Dark premonition crawled up Romeo's spine as he flipped to the next photo. It showed him walking out of his hotel and down the street that led to the trendy cafés near the waterfront.

He froze at the next picture and stared at the image of himself. And her.

Maisie O'Connell—the woman with the angelic face and the tempting, sinful body. The combination, although enthralling enough, wasn't what had made her linger in his mind long after he'd moved on to other women, and other experiences.

Something had happened with her in that hotel room, above and beyond mind-obliterating sex. He'd walked away from her feeling broken, fighting a yearning that had terrified him for a long time, until he'd finally forced it back under control.

He had no intention of resurrecting those brief, unsettling hours. He was in control of his life. In control of the fleeting moments of emotion he allowed himself these days.

He threw down the pictures, not caring when they fanned out in a careless arc on the desk. Eyes narrowed at Lorenzo, he snapped, 'It's almost laughable that you think documenting my sex life would cause me anything but acute irritation. Irritation that might just push me into having this house torn to the ground and the whole estate turned into a car park.'

The old man reached across, shuffled through the pictures, then sat back again.

Exhaling, Romeo looked down and saw more pictures of the woman he'd shared his most memorable one-night stand with. But these were different. Taken in another country, judging from the street signs. Dublin, most likely, where Maisie had said she was from during one of the brief times they'd conversed in that electric night they'd spent together.

Still caught up in riotous emotions, he nudged the picture impatiently with his fingernail.

Maisie O'Connell, striding down a busy street in a business suit and high heels, her thick, glorious hair caught up in an elaborate bun. A vision far removed from the sexy little sundress and flip-flops she'd been wearing the first time Romeo had seen her outside a waterfront café in Palermo. Her hair had been loose then, hanging to her waist in a ripple of dark fire.

Romeo unveiled the next picture.

Maisie, hailing a taxi outside a clinic, her features slightly pale and drawn, her normally bright blue eyes dark with worry.

Maisie, sitting on a park bench, her face turned up to the sun, her hand resting on her belly.

Her very distended belly.

Romeo swallowed hard and picked up the last picture, his body suspended in shock as he brought it up to his face.

Maisie, pushing a pram down a quiet Dublin street, her mouth tilted in a postcard-perfect picture of maternal bliss as she reached into the stroller.

'*Madre di Dio*, what is the meaning of this?' he breathed, his voice cold enough to chill the whole mausoleum of a mansion.

'I will not insult your deductive powers by spelling it out for you,' Lorenzo answered.

Romeo flung the photo down, but he could not look away from them. Spreading his fingers through the glossy images, he found further evidence of surveillance. Apparently his father had decided to stop following Romeo and focus instead on the woman he'd slept with on the day of his mother's funeral. A woman whose goodness had threatened to seep into him, to threaten the foundations of his carefully barricaded emotions.

'If these images are supposed to paint some sort of picture, then you've wasted your time. Sexually active individuals have brief encounters and go on to have relationships and families all the time. Or so I'm told.'

He'd never indulged in a relationship. In fact, he actively discouraged his lovers from even entertaining a glimmer of the idea. Romeo suppressed a grim smile. He knew his attitude to relationships had earned him the amusingly caustic label of *Weekend Lover*. Not that he cared. Hell, if it spelled out his intentions before he even asked a woman out, then all the better.

Affection was never on the table, the faintest idea of love strictly and actively forbidden. His interactions were about sex. Nothing more.

'So you don't care to know the time span during which these pictures were taken?'

'Fattore must have had his own warped reason, I'm sure.'

Lorenzo continued to stare at him. 'Then you won't want to know that the woman gave her child an Italian name?'

Romeo snorted in disbelief. He hadn't told Maisie his surname. He'd been very careful in that regard because he hadn't wanted any association with either his mother or his father discovered, as tenuous as the connection could've been, seeing that he hadn't set foot in Sicily in over fifteen years.

'You two must have been desperate to clutch at so many straws. My suggestion to you would be to leave this woman alone to raise her child. She means nothing to me other than a brief dalliance. Whatever leverage you seek through her has no teeth.'

Lorenzo shook his balding grey head. 'Once you have calmed down and learnt a little of our ways, you'll realise that we don't tend to leave stones unturned. Or facts unchecked. Your father certainly wouldn't pin the future of his organisation, of his *famiglia*, on a whim. No, *mio figlio*, we checked and double-checked our facts. Three DNA tests by three different doctors confirmed it.'

'How did you come by samples for these tests?'

'Contrary to what you think of us, we're not bumbling idiots. A strand of hair or a discarded juice cup is all we need, and quite easy to come by.'

The gross violation that deed would've entailed turned his stomach and primitive anger swelled through him. 'You set your thugs loose on a little boy?'

'He's not just any little boy. Your woman gave birth exactly nine months after your encounter. And your son is very much a Fattore.'

CHAPTER TWO

MAISIE O'CONNELL FLIPPED the Closed sign to Open and enjoyed the tingle of excitement that never failed to come with that little action.

It had been a long, hard slog, but *Maisie's* was finally ticking over very nicely, was making a steady profit, in fact. Putting her beloved restaurant in the hands of a professional chef while she'd taken the intensive course in gourmet Italian cooking had paid off. The added feature in one of Dublin's top newspapers had given *Maisie's* the extra boost that had seen her bookings go from half full to booked solid a month in advance.

Picking up the glass-topped menu stand, she pushed open the door and positioned it for maximum effect on the pavement.

As she turned to go back in, a stretch limo with blacked-out windows rolled by and stopped two doors down from where she'd paused. Maisie eyed the car. Although it wasn't strange for luxury cars to pass through the quiet little village of Ranelagh, seeing as they were close to Dublin city centre, the presence of this car caused a different sort of tingle. Telling herself she was being too fanciful, she swiped a dishcloth over the surface of the menu stand and went back in. She checked on her kitchen and waitstaff of twelve, made sure preparations were under way for their first booking at midday, then went into her office.

She had roughly half an hour to get to grips with the restaurant's accounts before she had to be back in the kitchen. As she sat down, her gaze fell on the picture propped up on her desk. The pulse of love that fired to her heart made her breath catch. Reaching out, she traced the contours of her son's face, her own face breaking into a smile at the toothy, wide-eyed happiness reflected in his eyes.

Gianlucca. The reason for her existence. The reason the hard decisions she'd made five years ago had been worth every moment of heartache. Turning her back on the career she'd trained so hard for had not been easy. Certainly her parents had piled on enough guilt to make walking away feel like the betrayal they'd accused her of committing. Her own guilt for confirming their fears that the apple didn't fall far from the tree was bone-deep and would probably always be. She hadn't planned on getting pregnant as her mother had at twenty-four but she refused to let the guilt prevent her from loving or caring for her child.

She'd known from a very young age that her parents, had they been given a choice, would've remained childless. As hard as it'd been, she'd tried to accept that not everyone was built to nurture a child. Her parents certainly had found raising her a challenge, one they hadn't deemed as worthy as the academic careers they'd pursued relentlessly. She'd always known she came an indifferent second to her parents' academic ambitions.

But she'd wanted Gianlucca the moment she'd found out he was growing inside her.

There had been nothing she wanted more than providing the very best for her son.

She had given him the very best.

The tiny niggle of ever-present guilt threatened to push its way through, but she smashed it down. She'd done everything she could when she'd found out she was pregnant. Even going against her parents' intense disapproval to make that daunting trip back to Sicily. She'd tried.

Yes, but did you try hard enough?

She dropped her hand from the picture and resolutely opened the account books. Indulging in *might have beens* wouldn't get the chequebook balanced or the staff paid. She was content enough. More important, her son was happy.

Her gaze drifted back to the almost-four-year-old face that was already taking the shape of the man he would one day be. To the deep hazel-gold eyes that looked so much like his father's. Eyes that could sometimes make her believe he could see straight into her soul, just as the older pair had done to her that long afternoon and longer night in Palermo five years ago.

Romeo.

A portentous name if there ever was one. While her life hadn't ended in fatal tragedy like the famous story, meeting Romeo had significantly altered it, her son being the only bright thing that had emerged from encountering that dangerously sexy, but deeply enigmatic Italian with eyes that had reflected enough conflict to last him several lifetimes.

Enough.

She switched on her computer and had just activated the payroll system when a knock sounded on her door.

'Come in.'

Lacey, her young reservations manager, poked her head around the door, her eyes wide and brimming with interest. 'There's someone here to see you,' she stage-whispered.

Maisie suppressed a smile. Her young employee had a flair for the dramatic and saw conspiracies and high drama in the simplest situations.

'If it's someone else looking for a job, please tell them I'm not hiring anyone. Not till the summer season really kicks off…' She stopped speaking as Lacey shook her head frantically.

'I don't think he's looking for a job. Actually, no offence, Maisie, but he looks like he could buy this place a hundred times over.' Her eyes widened and she blushed, then bit her lip. 'Sorry, but he looks really, really rich, and really, really, *intense*.' Lacey's eyes boggled some more. 'And he came in a *limo*,' she whispered again, looking over her shoulder into the restaurant.

The tingling Maisie had experienced earlier returned full force. 'Did he give you a name?'

'No, he just asked if you were in and ordered me to come and get you.' Lacey glanced furtively over her shoulder again, as if expecting their visitor to materialise behind her. 'He's very...*full-on*.'

Recalling her own line of thoughts moments ago and the intensity of Romeo's personality, she shivered. Shaking it off, Maisie stood up and brushed her hands down the practical black skirt and pink shirt she'd chosen to wear today.

She'd left all that dangerous intensity back in Palermo. Or *it* had left her, seeing as she'd woken up alone the morning after, with only rumpled sheets and the trace of her lover's scent on the pillow as evidence that she hadn't imagined the whole encounter.

She was in Ranelagh, the serene village she'd chosen to build a life for herself and her son in, not the sultry decadence of Palermo and its dangerous residents.

No danger or intensity whatsoever welcome here.

'Okay, Lacey. I'll take care of it.' Lacey's head bobbed before she disappeared from the doorway.

Sucking in a breath and telling herself she was being silly to feel so apprehensive, Maisie stepped out from behind her desk. In her short but successful stint as a criminal lawyer, she'd faced her share of unsavoury and even dangerous characters.

Whatever unknown quantity faced her out there in her beloved restaurant, she could face it.

Maisie knew just how wrong she was even before the tall, broad-shouldered figure clad from head to toe in black turned around from his brooding inspection of his surroundings.

Outwardly, her body froze a few steps into the restaurant. But inside, her heart kicked into her stomach. *Hard.*

'Romeo.'

She realised she'd said the name rattling through her brain aloud when he turned slowly and pinned her with those brooding hazel-gold eyes. That impossibly rugged jaw she'd thought she'd blown out of all proportion tightened as his gaze raked her from head to toe and back again. His prominent, cut-glass cheekbones were more pronounced than she remembered and his hair was longer, wavier than it had been five years ago. But the man who stood a dozen paces away was no less dynamic, no less captivating than the man who'd sat across from her in the café that memorable day.

If anything, he commanded a more overpowering presence. Perhaps it was because they were so far away from the place they'd first met, or because her mind was turning itself inside out to decipher exactly why he was here. All the same she found herself bunching a fist against her heart as if that would stop its fierce pounding.

'I'm not certain whether to celebrate this moment or to condemn it,' he rasped in a tense, dark voice.

'How did you… How did you find me?'

One eyebrow spiked upwards. 'That is what you wish to know? How did I find you? Were you attempting to stay hidden, perhaps?' he enquired silkily.

'What?' Her brain grew fuzzier, her heart racing even faster at the ice in his tone. 'I'm not hiding. Why would I want to hide from anyone?'

He approached slowly, his eyes not leaving her face, nor his hands the deep pockets of his overcoat. Even though it was early June, the weather remained cool enough to require a coat, and he wore his as a dark lord wore a cape, with a flourish that demanded attention. 'We haven't seen each other in five years and your first request is to know how I found you. Pardon me if I find that curious.'

'What would you have me say?' She licked lips gone

dry as he took another step closer until she had to crane her neck to see his eyes.

Mesmeric, hypnotising eyes.

So like his son's.

The blood drained from her face and thinking became difficult. She'd imagined this scene countless times. Had imagined how she would say the words. How he would take it. How she would protect her son from even the slightest hint of rejection, the way she'd done when her parents had transmitted that same indifference they'd shown Maisie all her life to her beloved son.

But words wouldn't form in her brain. So she stared at him, her thoughts twisting and turning.

'*Hello*, perhaps? Or, *how have you been, Romeo*?'

She caught his chillingly mocking tone and stiffened.

'Why would I? I seem to recall waking up to find myself alone in a hotel suite rented by an anonymous stranger. You didn't bother to say goodbye then, so why should I bother to say hello now?' she replied.

His nostrils flared then and a memory struck through her jumbled thoughts. They'd been caught up in one of the few short bursts of conversation in his suite. She'd unwittingly let slip the fraught state of her relationship with her parents, how lonely and inconvenient she felt to them, as if she were an unwanted visitor sharing a house with them.

His nostrils had flared then, too, as he'd admonished her to be grateful she had parents at all—strangers or otherwise. That observation had rendered her silent and a little ashamed, not because she'd hated being chastised, but because she'd seen the naked agony in his eyes when he'd said that. As if the subject of parents was one that terrorised him.

Maisie pushed the memory away and struggled to stay calm when he finally released her from his stare and looked around.

'What do you do here when you're not dabbling in being a restaurateur?' he asked.

She bristled. 'I'm not dabbling. I own this restaurant. It's my career.'

'Really? I thought you were a high-powered lawyer.'

She frowned. Had she told him that in Palermo? Back then she'd been newly qualified and working on exciting cases. Back then her parents had finally, grudgingly, accepted her career choice. She would even go as far as to consider that for the first time in her life she'd achieved something they were proud of, even if they hadn't quite been able to show it in the warm, loving way she'd seen her friends' parents exhibit.

Of course, they hadn't been thrilled that she'd announced soon after that she was taking a whole month off to travel Europe.

Despite her having the full support of her bosses to take the time off, her parents had advised her against the trip. Their utter conviction that stepping off the career ladder, even briefly, would ruin her life had finally confirmed how much they rued bringing a child, bringing *her*, into their lives.

And once she'd returned and told them she was pregnant...

Her heart caught at their bitter disappointment when she'd finally revealed her news. Roberta O'Connell hadn't needed to spell out that she thought Maisie had ruined her life for ever. It'd been clear to see. And knowing that by definition they thought having *her* had been a mistake had been an ache she hadn't been able to dispel.

Maisie shook her head to dispel the memory. 'No, not any longer. I gave up practising four years ago,' she answered Romeo.

He frowned. 'Why would you give up the job you trained so hard for?'

So she *had* told him more than she thought. Because how else would he know? And why was he questioning her like this, probing her for answers he already knew? Was he trying to trip her up somehow?

She swallowed. 'My priorities changed,' she replied crisply and stepped back. 'Now if you were just passing through and stopped to catch up, I really must get on. My first customers will be here shortly and I need to make sure the kitchen's ready to start the day.'

'You think I came all this way simply *to catch up*?' He looked around again, as if searching for something. Or someone.

Apprehension flowed like excess adrenaline through her blood, making her dizzy for a moment.

Romeo couldn't know about Gianlucca. Because *she'd* searched for him to no avail. No one else knew who the father of her child was. The only people who she would've confessed Romeo's identity to—her parents—hadn't wanted to know after she'd confessed to the one-night stand. Which was just as well because Maisie wouldn't have liked to confess that she hadn't known the surname of the man who'd impregnated her.

Maisie had a hard time accepting the fact that the only time her mother had initiated a heart-to-heart conversation had been to tell her to abandon her child's welfare to childminders and nannies. That her son, once he was born, should be left to others to raise, so Maisie could focus fully and solely on her career. There'd even been an offer of a fully paid boarding school once he was a toddler! Despite her knowing her parents' views on hands-on parenting, it'd still been harrowing to hear her mother's words, to know that had her parents had the choice when she was born, they'd have abandoned *her* to the same fate.

'I really don't know what you're doing here. But like I said, I need to be getting on—'

She gasped when he caught her upper arms in a firm, implacable hold.

'Where is he, Maisie? *Where is my son?*' he demanded, his voice a cold, deadly blade.

Several things happened at once. The door to the kitchen burst open and Lacey rushed through, just as the front door swung inward and a party of four walked in. The scene stopped in almost comical freeze-frame. No one moved except for Romeo, whose eyes narrowed as they went from the door to Lacey and then to Maisie's face.

When shock continued to hold her tongue prisoner, Romeo's lips compressed. Glancing at Lacey's name badge, he jerked his head imperiously. 'Lacey, you're in charge of reservations, yes?'

Lacey nodded, her wide-eyed look returning full force.

'Then see to the customers, *per favore*. Your boss and I will be in her office.'

Romeo marched her into the small room and shut the door behind him with a precise movement that suggested he was suppressing the need to slam it. Maisie was conquering equally intense emotions.

She put the width of her desk between them, then glared at him.

'I don't know who you think you are, but you can't walk in here and start bossing my employees about—'

'Deflecting won't help this situation. You know why I'm here. So let's dispense with trivialities. *Tell me where he is.*' That last remark was said with icy brevity that hammered a warning straight to her blood.

'Why?' she fired back, potent fear beginning to crawl up her spine.

Astonishment lit through his golden eyes. '*Why?* Are you completely insane? Because I want to see him.'

'Again, why?' A cloud descended on his face and Maisie held up her hand when he opened his mouth, no doubt to once again question her sanity. 'Let's stop for a moment and think about this rationally. We had a one-night stand.' She couldn't help the high colour that rushed into her face at the so very telling term. 'After which you walked away without so much as a thank-you-ma'am note. You used me, then disappeared into the night. A month later, I found out I was pregnant. Fast-forward five years later, you walk in the door and demand to see my son.' Maisie raised her hand and ticked off her fingers. 'I don't know your background. I don't know whether that aura of danger about you is just for show or the real thing. Hell, I don't even know your *last name*. And you think I should just expose you to my child?'

Several emotions flitted across his face—astonishment, anger, a touch of vulnerability that set her nape tingling, then grudging respect before settling into implacable determination.

He stared at her for a time, before he exhaled sharply. 'If the child is mine—'

She laughed in disbelief. 'Let me get this straight. You came here without even being sure that the child you're so desperate to see is yours?'

He folded his arms across his massive chest, the movement bunching his shoulders into even wider relief. Maisie became acutely aware of the room shrinking, and the very air being sucked up by his overwhelming presence. 'Since I've never met him, I cannot be one hundred per cent sure that he's mine, hence the request to see him. A man in my position has to verify allegations of fatherhood.'

Her eyes widened. 'Allegations? *Plural?* Are you saying this isn't the first time you've left a woman in a hotel room and found out there have been consequences to your actions?' Maisie wasn't sure why that stung so much. Had she imagined herself somehow unique? That a man who *looked* like him, kissed and made love as he had, would have limited the experience to her and only her? 'And what do you mean, a man in your position?'

Her barrage of questions caused his eyes to narrow further. 'You don't know who I am?'

'Would I be asking if I did?' she threw back. 'If you want

any semblance of cooperation from me, I demand to know your full name.'

His jaw flexed. 'My name is Romeo Brunetti.' The way he said it, the way he waited, as if the pronouncement should be accompanied by a round of trumpets and the clash of cymbals, set her spine tingling. When she didn't speak, a curious light entered his eyes. 'That means nothing to you?'

She shrugged. 'Should it?'

He continued to stare at her for another minute, before he shook his head and started to pace the small space in front of her desk. 'Not at all. So now we have our long-overdue introductions out of the way.'

Maisie cleared her throat. 'Mr Brunetti, I—' She froze as he let out a stunned breath.

Her gaze flew to his face to find his gaze transfixed on the photo on her desk. 'Is this... Is this him?' he asked in a tight, ragged whisper.

When she nodded, he reached forward in a jerky movement, then stopped. Apprehension slid over his face. He fisted and then flexed his hand, before he slowly plucked up the frame. In another person, she would've been certain he was borderline terrified of a mere picture.

Terrified or dreading?

The reminder of the cold indifference her parents had felt about their grandson, about her, made her itch to snatch the photo from him, protect her son's image the way she fought every day to keep him from the rejection she'd been forced to live with her whole life.

She glanced at the picture clutched in Romeo's large hand.

It had been taken at Ranelagh Gardens on the first day of spring. Dressed in a smart shirt, jeans and bright blue woollen jumper, Gianlucca had looked a perfect picture of health and happiness, and Maisie hadn't been able to resist capturing his image.

She watched now as Romeo brought the picture up close

to his face, his features drawn tight, his breathing slow and controlled. After almost a minute of staring at the photo without a hint of emotion, he raised his hand and brushed his fingers over Gianlucca's cheek, almost in direct imitation of what Maisie herself had done a mere half hour ago.

'*Mio figlio,*' he murmured.

'I don't know what that means,' Maisie replied in a matching whisper.

He blinked and sucked in a deep, chest-filling breath. 'My son. It means my son.' He looked up, his gaze deeply accusing. '*He's my son.* And you kept him from me,' he snarled, his voice still not quite as steady as it'd been moments ago.

Maisie stumbled backwards, bumping into the chair behind her. 'I did nothing of the kind. And if you stopped to think about it for a moment, you'd realise how ridiculous that allegation is.'

He shoved a hand through his thick dark hair, dislodging any semblance of order it'd been in. He began to pace again, the photo clutched in his large hand. 'How old is he?' he demanded when he paused for a moment.

'He's four in three weeks.'

He resumed pacing in tight circles. 'Four years... *Dio mio*, four years I've been in the dark,' he muttered to himself, slashing his hand through his hair again.

'How *exactly* were you enlightened?' It was a question he hadn't yet addressed.

He froze, as if her question had thrown him. 'We'll get to that in a moment. First, please tell me his name and where he is.'

The urgency in his voice bled through to Maisie. She wanted to refuse. Wanted to rewind time and have this meeting not happen. Not because being given the chance to reveal her son's existence to his father wasn't what she wanted.

From the moment she'd found out she was pregnant, she'd known she would give her child every opportunity to know his father. She'd gone to Palermo during her first trimester with that exact reason in mind and had given up after two weeks with no success in tracing Romeo.

No, the reason Maisie wanted to rewind time and take a different course was because she knew, deep in her bones, that Romeo's presence wasn't just about wanting to get to know his son. There was a quiet hint of danger about him that set her fear radar alight. And he hadn't yet shown her that the prospect of a son filled him with joy. All he'd done so far was put an alpha claim on a child he didn't know.

A child she would lay her life down to protect.

'Why are you really here?'

His brows clamped together. 'I believe we've tackled that particular question.'

She shook her head. Something was seriously, desperately wrong. Something to do with her precious son.

'No, we haven't. And I absolutely refuse to tell you anything about him until you tell me what's going on.'

CHAPTER THREE

ROMEO STARED DOWN at the picture one more time, his heart turning over as eyes the exact shade as his own stared back at him. The child...*his son*...was laughing, pure joy radiating from his face as he posed, chubby arms outstretched, for the camera. A deep shudder rattled up from his toes, engulfing him in a sense of peculiar bewilderment. And fear. Bone-deep fear.

He couldn't be a father. Not him, with the upbringing he'd had, the twisted, harrowing paths his life had taken before he'd wrestled control of it. He wasn't equipped to care for a dog, never mind a child. And with the blood flowing through his veins...the blood of a thug and a vicious criminal...

Dio mio.

Lorenzo hadn't been lying after all. A single wave of impotent rage blanketed him to know that the two men he despised most had known of the existence of the boy before he did. And while a part of him knew levelling accusations of subterfuge on the woman standing before him was unfair, Romeo couldn't help but feel bitter resentment for being kept in the dark, even while he continued to flounder at the reality stabbing him in the chest.

He pushed the emotion aside and concentrated on the reality he *could* deal with—her continued denial of access. Because whether he was equipped to handle the prospect of fatherhood or not, she was at this moment behaving like an irrational person...a mother bear—a concept acutely alien to him.

Inhaling deep to keep his emotions under control, he

rubbed his thumb over the face of his son. 'I have only just discovered I have a child.' He stopped when she raised her eyebrow again to remind him of her unanswered question. 'Through...business associates who wished to get my attention—'

She shook her head, her long ponytail swinging. 'What on earth does that mean? Why would business associates want to use your child to get your attention?' High colour had flown into her cheeks, reminding him of another time, another place when her emotions had run equally passionate. 'What type of business are you involved in?' she voiced suspiciously.

So she didn't know who he was. Something vaguely resembling relief speared through him. When his business partnership with Zaccheo Giordano had become public knowledge five years ago, his world had exploded with fawning acolytes and women falling over themselves to get his attention. That attention had increased a hundredfold when he'd opened his first super-luxury resort off the coast of Tahiti, a feat he'd repeated soon after with five more, seeing him skyrocket onto the World's Richest list.

It was curiously refreshing not to have to deal with the instant personality change that accompanied recognition of his name. But not refreshing enough to know his response had triggered suspicion that could keep him from his reason for being here. Even though her instinct might yet prove correct.

He needed to frame his words carefully.

'You have nothing to fear from me.' He'd managed to lock down his control after that gut punch he'd received on seeing her again. From here on in, he would be operating from a place of cold, hard intelligence.

She shook her head again. 'Sorry, that's not good enough. You'll have to do better than that.' Her gaze went to the picture frame he held on to, a fierce light of protection and possession burning in her striking blue eyes.

'Tell me the exact nature of your business or this conversation ends now.'

Romeo almost laughed. She was seriously deluded if she thought her heated threats would in any way dissuade him from seeing his son, from verifying for himself that the child truly belonged to him.

'I'm the CEO and owner of Brunetti International,' he replied.

She frowned for a moment, then her features morphed into astonishment. 'Brunetti...those resorts you need to sell an organ or a limb before you can afford a night there?'

He made a dismissive gesture. 'We cater to people from all walks of life.'

She snorted. 'As long as they've sold their grandmothers to be able to afford your billionaire rates.'

Romeo pursed his lips. His wealth wasn't the subject under discussion here.

The fact that she seemed to be a rare species, a mother who stood like a lioness in protection of her child, a child whom he'd yet to be certain without a shadow of a doubt shared his DNA, should take precedence.

'You know who I am now. You'll also know from your previous career that information can be discovered if one digs deep enough. My business associates dug deep enough and they found you and my son.'

'My son.'

The sudden urge to snarl *our child* took him by surprise. He stared down at the picture, clutching at the fraying edges of his control when he began to feel off balance again. '*Per favore.* Please. Tell me his name.'

Her gaze went to the picture and her features softened immediately.

The look was one he'd witnessed before, in that hotel room five years ago. It was a look that had set so many alarm bells ringing inside his head that he'd withdrawn swiftly and decisively from it. He looked away because just as he'd had no room to accommodate *feelings* then, he had no room for them now.

'His name is Gianlucca. Gianlucca O'Connell.'

An irrational surge of displeasure threatened to floor him. *'O'Connell?'*

Again that challenging arch of her eyebrow. Back in Palermo he'd seen her passion, her fire, but that had been directed to the bedroom, and what they'd done to each other in bed. Seeing it in a different light didn't make it any less sexy. Yet the punch of heat to his libido took him by surprise. He'd grown so jaded by the overabundance of willing women that lately he'd lost interest in the chase. For the past three months, work had become his mistress, the only thing that fired his blood in any meaningful way.

'That *is* my name. Or did you expect me to call him Gianlucca Romeo?'

He gritted his teeth. 'Did you even make an effort to find me when you knew you carried my child?'

A look crossed her face, a mixture of pride and anger, and she raised her chin. 'Did you want to be found?' she fired back.

Knowing how well he'd covered his tracks, a wave of heat crawled up his neck. He'd succeeded more than in his wildest dreams. He'd walked away, having effectively smashed down any residual feelings of rejection, or the idea that he could be worthy of something more than the brain and brawn that had seen him through his harrowing childhood into the man he was today.

The hours of imagined softness, of imagined affection, had been an illusion brought on by his mother's passing. An illusion he'd almost given in to. An emotion he'd vowed then never to entertain even the merest hint of again.

'We'll address the subject of his surname at another time. But now we've established who I am, I'd like to know more about him. Please,' he added when her stance remained intransigent.

'All I know is your surname. I don't even know how old you are, never mind what sort of man you are.'

Romeo rounded the desk and watched her back away, but looking into her eyes he saw no sign of fear. Only stubbornness. Satisfied that she didn't fear him, he moved closer, watched her pupils dilate as a different sort of chemistry filled the air. Her sudden erratic breathing told him everything he needed to know.

'I'm thirty-five. And five years ago, you gave yourself to me without knowing anything more about me besides my first name.' He watched a blush wash up her throat into her face with more than a little fascination. 'You were in a foreign place, with a strange man, and yet you trusted your instinct enough to enter my hotel suite and stay for a whole night. And right now, even though your heart is racing, you don't fear me. Or you would've screamed for help by now.' He reached out and touched the pulse beating at her throat. Her soft, silky skin glided beneath his fingertips and blazing heat lanced his groin again. Curbing the feeling, he dropped his hand and stepped back. 'I don't mean you or the boy harm. I just wish to see him. I deal in facts and figures. I need visual evidence that he exists, and as accommodating as I'm willing to be, I won't be giving you a choice in the matter.'

She swallowed, her eyes boldly meeting and staying on his. 'Just so you know, I don't respond well to threats.'

'It wasn't a threat, *gattina*.' They both froze at the term that had unwittingly dropped from his lips. From the look on her face, Romeo knew she was remembering the first time he'd said it. Her nails had been embedded in his back, her claws transmitting the depth of her arousal as he'd sunk deep inside her. His little wildcat had been as crazy for him as he'd been for her. But that was then, a moment in time never to be repeated. 'I'm merely stating a fact.'

She opened her mouth to reply, then stopped as voices filled the restaurant. 'I have to go. This is our busiest afternoon slot. I can't leave Lacey on her own.'

Romeo told himself to be calm. 'I need an answer, Maisie.'

She stared at him for a long moment before her gaze dropped to the picture he held. She looked as if she wanted to snatch it from him but he held on tight. She finally looked back up. 'He goes to playgroup from eleven to three o'clock. I take him to the park afterwards if the weather's good.'

'Did you have plans to do that today?'

She slowly nodded. 'Yes.'

Blood rushed into his ears, nearly deafening him. He forced himself to think, to plot the best way he knew how. Because rushing blood and racing hearts were for fools. Fools who let emotion rule their existence.

'What park?' he rasped.

'Ranelagh Gardens. It's—'

'I will find it.'

She paled and her hands flew out in a bracing stance. 'You can't… Don't you think we need to discuss this a little more?'

Romeo carefully set down the picture, then took out his phone and captured an image of it. He stared down at his son's face on his phone screen, and the decision concreted in his mind. 'No, Maisie. There's nothing more to discuss. If he's mine, truly mine, then I intend to claim him.'

Maisie slowly sank into the chair after Romeo made a dramatic exit, taking all the oxygen and bristling vitality of the day with him. She raised her hand to her face and realised her fingers were shaking. Whether it was from the shock of seeing him again after convincing herself she would never set eyes on him again, or the indomitability of that last statement, she wasn't certain.

She sat there, her hand on her clammy forehead, her gaze

in the middle distance as she played back every word, every gesture, on a loop in her mind.

The sound of laughter finally broke through her racing thoughts. She really needed to walk the floor, make sure her customers were all right. But she found herself clicking on her laptop, typing in his name on her search engine.

The images that confronted her made her breath catch all over again. Whereas she hadn't given herself permission to linger on anywhere but Romeo's face while they'd been in her office, she leaned in close and perused each image. And there were plenty, it seemed. Pictures of him dressed in impeccable handmade suits, posing for a profile piece in some glossy business magazine; pictures of him opening his world-renowned resorts in Dubai and Bali; and many, many pictures of him with different women, all drop-dead gorgeous, all smiling at him as if he was their world, their every dream come true.

But the ones that caught Maisie's attention, the ones that made her heart lurch wildly, were of Romeo on a yacht with another man—the caption named him as Zaccheo Giordano—and a woman with two children. The children were Gianlucca's age, possibly a little older, and the pictures were a little grainy, most likely taken with a telephoto lens from a long distance.

He sat apart from the family, his expression as remote as an arctic floe. That lone-wolf look, the one that said approach with caution, froze her heart as she saw it replicated in each rigid, brooding picture that followed. Even when he smiled at the children, there was a distance that spoke of his unease.

Trembling, Maisie sat back from the desk, the large part of her that had been agitated at the thought of agreeing to a meeting between Romeo and her son escalating to alarming proportions.

She might not know how he felt about children gener-ally, but if the pictures could be believed, Romeo Brunetti wasn't the warm and cuddly type.

Maisie gulped in the breath she hadn't been able to fully access while Romeo had been in the room and tried to think rationally. She'd tried to find Romeo five years ago to tell him that they'd created a child together. It was true that at the time she'd been reeling from her parents' further dis-appointment in her, and in hindsight she'd probably been seeking some sort of connection with her life suddenly in chaotic free fall. But even then, deep down, she'd known she couldn't keep the news to herself or abandon her baby to the care of strangers as her parents had wanted.

So in a way, this meeting had always been on the cards, albeit to be scheduled at a time of her choosing and without so much...pulse-destroying drama.

Or being confronted with the evidence that made her mothering instincts screech with the possibility that the father of her child might want him for reasons other than to cement a love-at-first-sight bond that would last a lifetime.

She clicked back to the information page and was in the middle of Romeo's worryingly brief biography when a knock announced Lacey's entrance.

'I need you, Maisie! A group of five just walked in. They don't have a booking but I don't think they'll take no for an answer.'

Maisie suppressed a sigh and closed her laptop with a guilty sense of relief that she didn't have to deal with Romeo's last words just yet.

'Okay, let's go and see what we can do, shall we?'

She pinned a smile on her face that felt a mile from genu-ine and left her office. For the next three hours, she pushed the fast-approaching father-and-son meeting to the back of her mind and immersed herself in the smooth running of the lunchtime service.

* * *

The walk to Gianlucca's nursery took less than ten minutes, but with her mind free of work issues, her heart began to race again at the impending meeting.

Every cell in her body urged her to snatch her son and take him far away.

But she'd never been the type to run, or bury her head in the sand.

She'd give Romeo the chance to spell out what he wished for, and if his parting remarks were anything to go by he would be demanding a presence in her son's life. She would hear him out, but nothing would make her accommodate visitation with her son until she was absolutely sure he would be safe with Romeo.

Her heart lurched at the thought that she'd have to part from him for a few hours maybe once or twice a week. Maybe a full weekend when he grew older. Her breath shuddered out, and she shook her head. She was getting ahead of herself. For all she knew, Romeo would take one look at Lucca, satisfy himself that he was his and ring-fence himself with money-grubbing lawyers to prevent any imagined claims.

But then, if that was what he intended, would he have taken the time to seek them out?

Whatever happened, her priority would remain ensuring her son's happiness. She stopped before the nursery door, unclenched her agitated fists and blinked eyes prickling with tears.

From the moment he'd been born, it'd been just the two of them. After the search for Romeo had proved futile, she'd settled into the idea that it would always be just the two of them.

The threat to that twosome made her insides quiver.

She brushed her tears away. By the time she was buzzed in, Maisie had composed herself.

'Mummy!' Gianlucca raced towards her, an effervescent bundle of energy that pulled a laugh from Maisie.

Enfolding him in her arms, she breathed his warm, toddler scent until he wriggled impatiently.

'Are we going to the park to see the ducks?' he asked eagerly, his striking hazel eyes—so like his father's it was uncanny—widened expectantly.

'Yes, I even brought some food for them,' she replied and smiled wider when he whooped and dashed off towards the door.

She spotted the limo the moment they turned into the square. Black and ominous, it sat outside the north entrance in front of an equally ominous SUV, both engines idling. Beside the limo, two men dressed in black and wearing shades stood, their watchful stance evidence that they were bodyguards.

Maisie tried not to let her imagination careen out of control. Romeo Brunetti was a billionaire and she'd dealt with enough unscrupulous characters during her stint as a lawyer to know the rich were often targets for greedy, sometimes dangerous criminals.

All the same, she clutched Gianlucca's hand tighter as they passed the car and entered the park. Gianlucca darted off for the duck pond, his favourite feature in the park, as soon as she handed him the bread she'd taken from the restaurant.

He was no more than a dozen paces away when a tingle danced on her nape. She glanced over her shoulder and watched Romeo enter the park, his gaze passing cursorily over her before it swung to Gianlucca.

Maisie's heart lurched, then thundered at the emotions that washed over his face. Wonder. Shock. Anxiety. And a fierce possessiveness that sent a huge dart of alarm through her.

But the most important emotion—love—was missing.

It didn't matter that it was perhaps irrational for her to

demand it of him, but the absence of that powerful emotion terrified her.

Enough to galvanise her into action when he walked forward, reached her and carried on going.

'Romeo!' She caught his arm when she sensed his intention.

'What?' He paused, but his gaze didn't waver from Gianlucca's excited form.

'Wait. Please,' she whispered fiercely when he strained against her hold.

He whirled to her, his nostrils flaring as he fought to control himself. 'Maisie.' His tone held a note of barely leashed warning.

Swallowing, she stood her ground. 'I know you want to meet him, but you can't just barge in looking like...' She stopped and bit her lip.

'Looking like what?'

'Like a charging bull on steroids. You'll frighten him.'

His face hardened and he breathed deep before spiking a hand through his hair. After another long glance at Gianlucca, he faced her. '*Bene*, what do you suggest?'

Maisie reached into her bag. 'Here, I brought one of these for you.'

He eyed her offering and his eyebrows shot up. 'A bag of dried bread?'

'He's feeding the ducks. It's his favourite thing to do. I thought you could...approach him that way.'

Romeo's eyes darkened to a burnished gold. Slowly, he reached out and took the offering. *'Grazie,'* he muttered with tight aloofness.

She held on when he started to turn away, silently admonishing herself for experiencing a tiny thrill of pleasure when his arm flexed beneath her fingers. 'Also, I'd prefer it if you didn't tell him who you are. We can have a longer discussion about where we go from here before anything happens.'

A dark look gleamed in his eyes, but he nodded. 'If that is what you wish.'

'It is.'

He nodded, then tensed as a trio of kids flew by on their way to the pond. 'I agree, perhaps this isn't the most appropriate venue for an introduction.'

A tight knot eased in Maisie's stomach and she realised a part of her had feared Romeo would only want to see his son from afar and decide he didn't want to know him. She had yet to decipher his true motives, but she would allow this brief meeting.

'Thank you.'

He merely inclined his head before his gaze swung back to Gianlucca. Knowing she couldn't postpone the meeting any longer, she fell into step beside Romeo.

Gianlucca threw the last of his bread into the waiting melee of ducks and swans and broke into a delighted laugh as they fought over the scraps. His laughter turned into a pout when the ducks swam off to greet the bread-throwing trio of kids. 'Mummy, more bread!' When Maisie remained silent, he turned and raced towards them. 'Please?' he added.

She glanced at Romeo and watched the frozen fascination on his face as Gianlucca reached them. She caught him before he barrelled into her and crouched in front of him. 'Wait a moment, Lucca. There's someone I want you to meet. This...this is Romeo Brunetti.'

Lucca tilted his head up and eyed the towering man before him. 'Are you Mummy's friend?'

Romeo's head bobbed once. 'Yes. Nice to meet you, Gianlucca.'

Gianlucca immediately slipped his hand into Romeo's and pumped with all his might. A visible tremble went through Romeo's body, and he made a strangled sound. Gianlucca heard it and stilled, his eyes darting from the giant man to his mother.

The overprotective mother in her wanted to scoop him up and cuddle him close, but Maisie forced herself to remain still. Her breath caught as Romeo sank into a crouch, still holding his son's hand, his eyes glistening with questions.

'I look forward to getting to know you, Gianlucca.'

Lucca nodded, then gasped as he saw what Romeo held in his other hand. 'Did you come to feed the ducks, too?'

Romeo nodded. '*Sì*…yes,' he amended and started to rise. His body bristled with a restlessness that made Maisie's pulse jump. 'That was my intention, but I'm not an expert, like you.'

'It's easy! Come on.' He tugged at Romeo's hand, his excitement at having another go at his favourite pastime vibrating through his little body.

Maisie stayed crouched, the residual apprehension clinging to her despite the sudden, throat-clogging tears. As meetings between father and son went, it had gone much easier than she could've hoped for. And yet, she couldn't move from where she crouched. Because, she realised, through all the scenarios she'd played in her mind, she'd never really thought beyond this moment. Oh, she'd loftily imagined dictating visitation terms and having them readily agreed to, and then going about raising her son with minimal interference.

But looking at Romeo as he gazed down at his son with an intense proprietary light in his eyes, Maisie realised she really had no clue what the future held. Her breath shuddered out as Romeo's words once again flashed through her brain.

There's nothing more to discuss. If he's mine, truly mine, then I intend to claim him.

She slowly rose and looked over her shoulder. Sure enough, the two black-clad bodyguards prowled a short distance away. About to turn away, Maisie froze as she spotted two more by the south gate. Two more guarded the west side of the park.

Heart in her throat, she approached the duck pond, where Romeo was throwing a piece of bread under her son's strict instruction.

His head swung towards her and his expression altered at whatever he read on her face. 'Something wrong?'

'I think I should be asking you that,' she hissed so Gianlucca wouldn't overhear, but she placed a protective hand on his tiny shoulder, ready to lay down her life for him if she needed to. 'Do you want to tell me why you have *six* bodyguards watching this park?' Her voice vibrated with the sudden fear and anger she couldn't disguise.

His face hardened and the arm he'd raised to throw another bite into the pond slowly lowered to his side. 'I think it's time to continue this conversation elsewhere.'

CHAPTER FOUR

ROMEO WATCHED SEVERAL expressions chase over her face.

'What does that mean?' she asked, her blue eyes narrowing before she cast another alarmed glance at the burly men guarding the park.

He followed her apprehensive gaze and indicated sharply at his men when he saw that other parents were beginning to notice their presence. The men melted into the shadows, but the look didn't dissipate from Maisie's face. When her hand tightened imperceptibly on Gianlucca's shoulder, Romeo's insides tightened.

'My hotel is ten minutes away. We'll talk there.' He tried not to let the irony of his statement cloud the occasion. He'd said similar words to her five years ago, an invitation that had ended with him reeling from the encounter.

That invitation had now brought him to this place, to his son. He had no doubt in his mind that the child was his. Just as he had no doubt that he would claim him, and protect him from whatever schemes Lorenzo had up his sleeves. Beyond that, he had no clue what his next move was. He didn't doubt, though, that he would find a way to triumph. He'd dragged himself from the tough streets of Palermo to the man he was today. He didn't intend to let anything stand in the way of what he desired.

He focused to find her shaking her head. 'I can't.'

Romeo's eyes narrowed as a hitherto thought occurred to him. 'You can't? Why not?' He realised then how careless he'd been. Because Lorenzo's pictures had shown only Maisie with his son, Romeo had concluded that she was unattached. But those pictures were four years old. A lot could have happened in that time. She could've taken another lover, a man who had perhaps become important enough to see himself as Gianlucca's father.

The very idea made him see red for one instant. 'Is there someone in your life?' He searched her fingers. They were ringless. But that didn't mean anything these days. 'A *lover*, perhaps?' The word shot from his mouth like a bullet.

Her eyes widened and she glanced down at Gianlucca, but he was engrossed in feeding the last of the bread to the ducks. 'I don't have a lover or a husband, or whatever the *au fait* term is nowadays.'

Romeo attributed the relief that poured through him to not having to deal with another tangent in this already fraught, woefully ill-planned situation. 'In that case there shouldn't be a problem in discussing this further at my hotel.'

'That wasn't why I refused to come with you. I have a life to get on with, Romeo. And Lucca has a schedule that I try to keep to so his day isn't disrupted, otherwise he gets cranky. I need to fix his dinner in half an hour and put him to bed so I can get back to the restaurant.'

He stiffened. 'You go to work after he's asleep?'

Her mouth compressed. 'Not every night, but yes. I live above the restaurant and my assistant manager lives in the flat next door. She looks after him on the nights I work.'

'That is unacceptable.'

Her eyes widened with outrage. 'Excuse me?' she hissed.

'From now on you will not leave him in the care of strangers.'

Hurt indignation slid across her face. 'If you knew me at all, you'd know leaving my son with some faceless stranger is the last thing I'd do! Bronagh isn't a stranger. She's my friend as well as my assistant. And how dare you tell me how to raise my son?'

He caught her shoulders and tugged her close so they wouldn't be overheard. 'He is *our* son,' he rasped into her ear. 'His safety and well-being have now become my concern as much as yours, *gattina*.' The endearment slipped out again, but he deemed it appropriate, so he didn't allow the tingle that accompanied the term to disturb him too much. 'Put your claws away and let's take him back to your flat. You'll feed him and put him to bed and then we'll talk, *si*?'

He pulled back and looked down at her, noting her hectic colour and experiencing that same punch to his libido that had occurred earlier.

Dio, he needed this added complication like a bullet in the head.

He dropped his hand once she gave a grudging nod.

'Lucca, it's time to go,' she called out.

'One more minute!' came his son's belligerent reply.

A tight, reluctant smile curved Maisie's lips, drawing Romeo's attention to their pink plumpness. 'He has zero concept of time and yet that's his stock answer every time you try to get him away from something he loves doing.'

'I'll bear that in mind,' he answered.

He glanced at his son and that sucker-punch feeling slammed into him again. It'd first happened when Gianlucca had slid his hand into his. Romeo had no term for it. But it was alive within him, and swelling by the minute.

Unthinking questions crowded his mind. Like when had Gianlucca taken his first step? What had been his first word?

What was his favourite thing to do besides feeding greedy ducks?

He stood, stock-still, as a plan began to formulate at the back of his mind. A plan that was uncharacteristically outlandish.

But wasn't this whole situation outlandish in the extreme?

And hadn't he learned that sometimes it was better to fight fire with fire?

The idea took firmer root, embedding itself as the only

viable course available to him if he was to thwart the schemes of Lorenzo Carmine and Agostino Fattore.

The more Romeo thought about the plans the old men, in their bid to hang on to their fast-crumbling empire, had dared to lay out for him, the more rage threatened to overcome him. He'd tempered that rage with caution, not forgetting that a wounded animal was a dangerous animal. Fattore's lieutenant might be old, and his power weakened, but Romeo knew that some power was better than no power to people like Lorenzo. And they would hang on to it by every ruthless means available.

Romeo didn't intend to lower his guard where Lorenzo's wily nature was concerned. His newly discovered son's safety was paramount. But even if Lorenzo and the shadows of Romeo's past hadn't been hanging over him, he would still proceed with the plan now fully formed in his mind.

He followed Maisie as she approached and caught up Gianlucca's hand. 'Time to go, precious.' The moment he started to protest, she continued, 'Which do you prefer for your tea, fish fingers or spaghetti and meatballs?'

'Spaghetti balls,' the boy responded immediately, his mind adeptly steered in the direction of food, just as his mother had intended. He danced between them until they reached the gate.

Romeo noticed his men had slipped into the security SUV parked behind his limo and nodded at the driver who held the door open. He turned to help his son into the car and saw Maisie's frown.

'Do you happen to have a car seat in there?' she asked.

Romeo cursed silently. 'No.'

'In that case, we'll meet you back at the restaurant.' She turned and started walking down the street.

He shut the door and fell into step beside her. 'I'll walk back with you.'

She opened her mouth to protest but stopped when he

took his son's hand. The feel of the small palm against his tilted Romeo's world.

He hadn't known or expected this reality-changing situation when he'd walked into that mansion in Palermo yesterday. But Romeo was nothing if not a quick study. His ability to harness a situation to his advantage had saved his life more times on the street than he could recount. He wasn't in a fight-to-the-death match right now, but he still intended to emerge a winner.

Maisie's first priority when she'd decorated her flat was homey comfort, with soft furnishings and pleasant colours to make the place a safe and snug home for her son. But as she opened the door and walked through the short hallway that connected to the living room she couldn't help but see it through Romeo's eyes. The carpet was a little worn, one cushion stained with Lucca's hand paint. And suddenly, the yellow polka-dot curtains seemed a little too bright, like something a *girlie* girl would choose, instead of the sophisticated women Romeo Brunetti probably dated.

What did it matter?

She turned, prepared to show her pride in her home, and found him frozen in front of the framed picture collage above her TV stand. Twelve pictures documented various key stages of Lucca's life so far, from his scrunched-up hours-old face to his first Easter egg hunt two months ago.

Romeo stared at each one with an intensity that bordered on the fanatic. Then he reached out and traced his fingers over Lucca's first picture, the tremor in his hand hard to miss.

'I have digital copies…if you'd like them,' she ventured.

He turned. The naked emotion in his eyes momentarily stopped her breath.

'*Grazie*, but I don't think that would be necessary.'

Her heart stopped as the fear she hadn't wanted to fully

explore bloomed before her eyes. 'What does that mean?' she asked, although she risked him further exploiting the rejection he'd just handed her.

'It means there are more important things to discuss than which pictures of my son I would like copies of.'

Lucca chose that moment to announce his hunger.

Maisie glanced at Romeo, questions warring with anger inside her.

She didn't want to leave her son now that she knew Romeo was preparing to back away. Especially since there was also the outside threat evidenced by the bodyguards in the SUV that had crawled behind them as they'd walked back. He travelled with too much security for a garden-variety billionaire.

That knowledge struck fear into her heart that she couldn't dismiss.

'Go and make his meal, Maisie,' Romeo said.

The taut command in his voice jerked her spine straight.

'I'd rather take him into the kitchen with me.'

'Is that your normal routine?' he queried with narrowed eyes.

'No, normally he likes to watch his favourite children's TV show while I cook.'

Romeo gave a brisk nod. 'Go, then. I'll find a way of entertaining him,' he replied.

'What do you know about entertaining children?' she demanded fiercely.

His jaw clenched. 'Even rocket science has been mastered. Besides, you'll be in the next room. What could go wrong?'

Everything.

The word blasted through her head. She opened her mouth to say as much but saw Lucca staring with keen interest at them. The last thing she wanted was for her son to pick up the dangerous undercurrents in the room.

Romeo watched her for a minute, clench-jawed. 'Are there any other exits in the flat, besides the front door?'

Maisie frowned. 'There's a fire escape outside my bedroom.'

'Is it locked?'

'Yes.'

'Okay.' He strode out and she followed him into the hallway. She watched him lock and take out the key and return to her. 'Now you can be assured that I won't run off with him while your back is turned. I'll also keep conversation to a minimum so I don't inadvertently verbally abuse him. Are you satisfied?'

Her fingers curled around the key, and she refused to be intimidated. 'That works. I won't be long. The meatballs are already done... I just need to cook the pasta.'

Romeo nodded and looked to where Lucca knelt on the floor surrounded by a sea of Lego. He shrugged off his overcoat and draped it over the sofa. Maisie watched him advance towards Lucca, his steps slow and non-threatening, to crouch next to him.

Lucca looked up, smiled and immediately scooped up a handful of Lego and held it out to him.

Maisie backed out, fighting the tearing emotions rampaging through her. Admonishing herself to get her emotions under control, she rushed into the kitchen and set about boiling water for the spaghetti, all the while trying to dissect what the presence of the bodyguards meant.

Surely if Romeo was in some sort of trouble the Internet search would've picked it out? Or was she blowing things out of proportion? Was she wrong about billionaires travelling with that much security? She frowned at the total excess of it. And what about Romeo's explanation that his business associates had found Lucca? From her time as a lawyer, Maisie knew deep background checks had become par for the course during business deals, but from Romeo's expression in the park, she couldn't help feeling there was more.

Her heart hammered as horrific possibilities tumbled through her mind. The world was a dangerous place. Even in a picturesque haven like Ranelagh, she couldn't guarantee that she would always be able to keep Lucca safe.

She froze at the sink. Had she invited danger in by letting Romeo Brunetti through her front door? Or had he been right when he'd told her she'd instinctively trusted him in Palermo or she'd never have gone up to his suite that day?

She must have on some level, surely, or she'd never have given him her virginity so easily.

Stop!

The only way to find out what was going on was to talk to Romeo. That wouldn't happen unless she stopped dawdling and got on with it.

She fixed Lucca's meal and set it up in the dining nook attached to her kitchen. Seeing Romeo sprawled on his side on the living-room floor stopped her in her tracks. Between father and son, they'd built a giant castle and were debating where to station the knights, with Lucca in favour of ground sentry duty and Romeo advocating turret guards.

He sensed her watching and looked up. Again Maisie was struck by the determination on his face.

And again, he shuttered the look and handed the knight to Lucca.

Maisie cleared her throat before she could speak. 'Lucca, your food's ready.'

'One more minute!'

Romeo lifted an eyebrow and gave a mock shudder. 'Do you enjoy cold spaghetti, Gianlucca?'

Lucca shook his head. 'No, it tastes yucky.'

'Then I think you should eat yours now before it turns yucky, *sì*?'

'See what?' Lucca asked, his eyes wide and enquiring.

Romeo reached out and hesitantly touched his son's hair. '*Sì* means yes in Italian,' he said gruffly.

'Are you Ita…Itayan? Mummy said I'm half Itayan.'

Romeo's eyes flicked to Maisie for a moment, then returned to his son. 'Yes, she's right. She's also waiting for you to go eat your dinner.' A quiet, firm reminder that brought Lucca to his feet.

He whizzed past her and climbed into his seat at the small dining table. He barely waited for Maisie to tuck his bib into place before he was tearing into his spaghetti.

Romeo leaned against the doorjamb, a peculiar look on his face as he absorbed Lucca's every action.

Then he turned and looked at her, and her heart caught. Nothing could keep down the geyser of apprehension that exploded through her at what that absorbed look on Romeo's face meant for her and her son.

In that moment, Maisie knew that nothing she said or did would stop what was unravelling before her eyes. It didn't matter whether Romeo loved his son or not, he would do exactly as he'd said in her office this morning.

Romeo Brunetti had every intention of claiming his son.

Maisie entered the living room and paused to watch Romeo's broad frame as he looked out of the window at the street below. With the endless horrific thoughts that had been tumbling through her mind for the past three hours, she wondered if he was just pavement-watching or if there was some unseen danger lurking out there.

He turned and her breath caught at the intensity in his face, the dangerous vibe surrounding his body. Wanting to get this over with quickly, she walked further into the living room.

'He's out like a light. When he's worn out like that, he won't wake until morning.' Maisie wondered why she'd been dropping little morsels like this all evening. Then she realised it was because Romeo voraciously lapped up each titbit about his son.

Because a part of her hoped that, by doing so, she could get him to rethink whatever he was plotting for Lucca's future? Did she really think she could turn Romeo's fascination with their son into love?

Love couldn't be forced. Either it was there or it wasn't. Her parents had been incapable of it. They'd cared only for their academic pursuits and peer accolades. None of that love had spilled to her.

She balled her fists. She would rather Romeo absented himself completely than dangle fatherhood in front of her son, only to reject him later. 'You wanted to talk?' she ventured. The earlier they laid things out in the open, the quicker she could get back to the status quo.

Romeo nodded in that solemn way he sometimes did, then remained silent and still, his hands thrust into his pockets. He continued to watch her, dark hazel eyes tracking her as she straightened the cushions and packed away the toys.

Too soon she was done. Silence filled the room and her breath emerged in short pants as she became painfully aware that they were alone, that zing of awareness spreading wider in the room.

She realised she was fidgeting with her fingers and resolutely pulled them apart. 'I don't mean to hurry this along, but can we just get it over—'

'Sit down, Maisie.'

She wanted to refuse. Just on principle because she wouldn't be ordered about in her own home, but something in his face warned her she needed to sit for what was coming.

Heart slamming into her ribcage, she perched on the edge of the sofa. He took the other end, his large body turned towards her so their knees almost touched. Again awareness of just how big, how powerfully built he was, crowded her senses. Her gaze dropped to his hands, large with sleek fingers. She recalled how they'd made her feel, how the light dusting of hair on the back had triggered delicious shivers in her once upon a time.

A different tremble powered up her spine.

Maisie gave herself a silent shake. This wasn't the time to be falling into a pool of lust. She'd been there, done that, with this man. And look where it had got her.

Look where she was now, about to be given news she instinctively knew would be life-changing.

She glanced up at him. His hazel eyes probed, then raked her face, and his nostrils flared slightly, as if he, too, was finding it difficult to be seated so close to her without remembering what they'd done to each other on a hot September night in Palermo five years ago. His gaze dropped to her throat, her breasts, and she heard his short intake of breath.

'Romeo...'

He balled his fists on top of his thighs and his chest expanded in a long inhalation. 'You're right about the bodyguards. I normally only travel with two members of my security team.'

Her stomach hollowed out. 'Why...why the increase?'

'It's just a precaution at this stage.'

'What does that mean?' she demanded. 'Precaution against what?'

'It means neither you nor Gianlucca are in danger at the moment.'

'But you're expecting us to be at some point?' Her voice had risen with her escalating fear and the shaking had taken on a firmer hold.

He shook his head. 'You don't need to panic—'

'Oh, really? You tell me my son could be in danger and then tell me not to panic?' she blurted, all the different scenarios she'd talked herself out of tumbling back again. She brushed her hands over her arms as cold dread drowned her.

'I meant, there was no need to panic because I'll ensure your safety,' he said.

'Safety from what?' When he remained silent, she jumped to her feet and paced the small living room. 'I think you should start from the beginning, Romeo. Who are these people and what do they want with you? With our son?'

She froze. 'Are you involved in…in criminal activity?' she whispered in horror.

His mouth compressed and his face set into harsh, determined lines. 'No, I am not.'

The scathing force of the words prompted her to believe him. But the fear didn't dissipate. 'Please tell me what's going on.'

He rose, too, and paced opposite her. When his fists clenched and unclenched a few times, she approached. At the touch of her hand on his arm, he jerked, as if he'd been elsewhere.

As he stared down at her, his mouth compressed. 'My past isn't what you'd call a white-picket-fence fairy tale,' he said obliquely.

Maisie attempted a smile. 'Only the books I read to Lucca contain those. Real life is rarely that way.'

A grim smile crossed his lips. 'Unfortunately, mine was a little more dire than that.'

She kept quiet, mostly because she didn't know how to respond.

'The man whose blood runs through my veins was the head of a Sicilian organised crime family.'

She gasped, then stepped back as the import of the words sank in. 'You're a member of a Mafia gang?'

'No, I'm not.' Again that scathing denial.

'But your…your father is?'

'He wasn't my father. We just share the same DNA,' he bit out in a harsh tone that spoke of anger, bitterness and harrowing pain.

Maisie's eyes widened. As if aware of how he'd sounded, Romeo breathed deeply and slid his fingers through his hair. 'The abbreviated story is that I met him twice. Both times ended…badly. What I didn't know until yesterday was that he'd kept tabs on me all my life.'

'Why?' she demanded.

Romeo shrugged. 'Since I didn't know the man, I can

only guess it was some sort of power-trip thing to watch whether I failed or succeeded. Or it may have been for other reasons. I care very little about what his motives were.'

Maisie frowned. 'You talked about him in the past tense…because…'

'He and his family died in a yacht explosion a year ago.'

The rush of blood from her head made her light-headed. 'Was it an accident?' she asked, her lips numb.

His mouth pursed for a few seconds before he answered, 'Officially. But probably not.'

Her gasp brought his head up. Cursing under his breath, he strode to her and grasped her arms. 'I'm only going by what my gut tells me, Maisie. I don't have hard evidence to the contrary.'

'And your gut tells you he was assassinated?'

He nodded.

A million more questions crowded her brain, but she forced a nod. 'Go on.'

His hands moved to her shoulders, a firm glide that left a trail of awareness over her skin. 'I received a letter from his lawyers a month ago, summoning me to Palermo, which I ignored. I received a few more after that. The last one told me he'd left me something I needed to collect in person.' His mouth twisted. 'My curiosity got the better of me.'

'What was it?'

'His monstrosity of a mansion. Along with his plans for my future.'

Ice slithered down her spine. 'What plans?'

One hand moved to her neck and cupped her nape. The familiarity of that gesture thawed the ice a little, replacing her terror with a wave of warm awareness.

'He never had a son…not a legitimate one anyway. I think somewhere along the line he intended to contact me, bring me into the *family business*. He just never got the chance to. But he told his second in command about it. He was the one who asked the lawyers to contact me.'

'What does he want from you?'

'The *famiglia* is falling apart. They need a new injection of young blood, and an even greater need for an injection of financial support.'

'You have both.'

'But I intend to give them neither.'

Maisie stared at his granite-hard face, the deep grooves bracketing his mouth and the dark gold of his eyes, and the pennies finally tumbled into place. 'But if you don't intend to... Oh, my God. You think they mean to use Lucca to make you do what they want?' she rasped in a terror-stricken voice.

His grip tightened and one finger caught her chin and raised her face to his spear-sharp gaze. Her stomach knotted at the savage determination on his face. 'They will *never* get their hands on you or our son. You have my word on this, Maisie.'

She shook her head, her insides growing colder by the second. 'But you can't guarantee that, can you? Or you wouldn't be here with *six* bodyguards in tow.'

'There's one way to ensure your safety,' he said, his gaze raking her face as if he wanted to pull the answer from her even before he'd asked the question.

'What's that?' she murmured.

'You will marry me. Then you and our son will know the protection of my name.'

CHAPTER FIVE

SHE WENT HOT, then cold, then colder. Until she felt as brittle as chilled glass. Dumbly, she stared into those burnished gold eyes, sure she'd misheard him.

'What did you say?'

'The *famiglia* isn't as powerful as it once was, but I'm not willing to dismiss them out of hand, either. Marrying me will grant you and Lucca protection, which you could be vulnerable without.'

'No way. I can't…I can't just *marry* you! We know next to nothing about each other.'

A look curled through his eyes. 'Our circumstances aren't commonplace. Besides, we've already done things a little out of sequence, don't you think?'

She laughed, but the sound was more painful than she wanted it to be. 'This is far from a quaint little romantic caper.'

He nodded. '*Sì*, which is why I want to ensure I have all the bases covered for your protection.'

'Oh, God!'

'Maisie—'

'No.' She pulled out of his hold and backed away. 'This is preposterous. You have to find another way to protect Lucca.'

Golden eyes bored into hers. 'There's no other way. There's an unspoken code, *gattina*. They may be thugs, but they respect family. Marrying me means you and Lucca become off limits.'

'But it still won't be a cast-iron guarantee, will it?'

He shrugged. 'Nothing in life is guaranteed. I have no

intention of involving myself in that life, but there may be resistance. A temporary marriage is our best option.'

The cold pronunciation chilled her to the bone. She kept backing away until her shoulders nudged the window. Unrelenting, he prowled towards her.

'No way. I can't do it, Romeo. I just… I can't just fold up my life and uproot my son to live goodness knows where, looking over my shoulder every day!'

'Look!' He reached her, grasped her shoulders and turned her around, directing her gaze to the street, where his men maintained a watchful guard. 'Is this how you want Lucca to live? Surrounded by men in black carrying guns? Can you honestly say that you'll experience a moment of peace in the park, knowing that his life could be in danger from unknown elements at each second of the day?'

She shuddered. 'That's not fair, Romeo.'

His bitter laugh scoured her skin. 'Life's *never* fair, *gattina*,' he whispered in her ear. 'Believe me, I have firsthand experience in just how unfair life can be. That's why I want this for our son. He will bear my name, legitimately, and my protection.'

'But you *cannot* guarantee that, can you? Can't you just go to the authorities and tell them about this?'

He levelled a deep sigh. '*Sì*, I can. My lawyers have been apprised of what's going on. But, technically, Lorenzo hasn't committed a crime yet, just issued veiled threats. Even when he does, the wheels of justice don't always move fast, Maisie. You of all people should know that.'

Sadly, she knew that all too well. Nevertheless, she couldn't give what he was suggesting any room to grow. That a part of her wanted to let it grow deeply unnerved her. 'We can still—'

'We can do a lot of things.' He reached for her again, pinning her arms to her sides. 'None would be as effective as what I'm proposing. At the very least, it'll buy time until I can find another solution.'

She pulled away. She thought of her parents, of the frosty existence she'd lived with. Her parents' lack of warmth hadn't just been directed at her. They'd been equally frosty to each other. As she'd grown up, she'd realised that the only reason they'd married and stayed married had been because of her. A shiver of horror raked her from head to toe at the thought of placing herself in a similar arrangement. Lucca was sharp. It would be a matter of time before he sensed that his parents didn't love one another. The thought of what it would do to him made her recoil.

'Maisie—'

'No!' she cried. The part of her that hadn't been freaking out completely threw up its arms and buckled beneath the part that was exploding with hysteria. 'I won't do it! I won't—'

She gasped as strong arms clamped around her and she was hauled into his body.

'*Basta!* There's no need to get hysterical.'

She fought to free herself, but his arms tightened their hold on her. 'I'm not getting hysterical,' she lied. Inside, she was going out of her mind with information overload. And being this close to Romeo, feeling his taut, warm body against hers, wasn't helping, either. Planting her hands on his chest, she pushed. 'Let me go, Romeo!'

'Calm down, then I will.'

She stilled, then made the mistake of glancing up at him.

His eyes were molten, his lips parted slightly as he stared down at her. The look on his face morphed to replicate the dangerous sensations climbing through her.

'No...' she whispered.

'No,' he agreed roughly. And yet his head started to descend, his arms gathering her even closer until her breasts were pressed against his chest.

A second later, his hot, sensual mouth slanted over hers, and she was tumbled headlong into a different quagmire.

Only, this one contained no fear, no horror. Only an electrifying sizzle that rocked her from head to toe.

His tongue breached her mouth, his teeth biting along the way. Maisie whimpered as sensation engulfed her. She opened her mouth wider, her tongue darting out to meet his.

He groaned and pulled her closer. One hand fisted her hair, angled her head for a deeper penetration, while the other slid down her back to cup her bottom. He squeezed and yanked her into his hardening groin. As if a torch paper had been lit between them, Maisie scoured her hands over him, trailing his shoulders, his back, the trim hardness of his waist before her fingers dug into the tightness of his buttocks.

A rough sound exploded from his lips as he rocked against her pelvis, imprinting his erection against her belly in a clear demand that made her moan. Hunger she'd taught herself to bury suddenly reared up, urgent and demanding. When his hand cupped her breast and toyed with her nipple, Maisie wanted to scream, *Take me!*

But even that sound would have taken too much effort, drugged as she was by the power of his kisses. Her fingers trailed back up, curled into his hair as she gave herself over to the sensation drowning her.

'*Gattina*…my little wildcat,' he groaned once he'd lifted his head to trail kisses along her jaw.

Maisie moaned as he bit her earlobe. 'Romeo.' Her speech was slurred and the secret place between her legs lit on fire from wanting him. From wanting her hunger assuaged.

He recaptured her mouth and Maisie was certain she would die just from the pleasure overload.

'Mummy!'

They exploded apart, their breaths erratic and ragged as they stared at each other across the space between them.

Romeo looked dazed, hectic colour scouring his cheekbones, his golden eyes hot and brooding and alive with arousal. She suspected she wore the same look, if not worse.

'Mummy!'

She lurched, still dazed, towards the door leading out into the hallway.

'Gattina.'

She didn't want to hear that term, didn't want to be reminded that she'd behaved like a horny little hellcat with her son asleep two doors away. But she turned anyway, met that torrid, golden gaze.

'Fix your shirt,' he rasped throatily.

Maisie looked down at the gaping shirt exposing her chest. The buttons had come undone without her having the vaguest idea when it'd happened. Flushing, she shakily secured them and hurried to her son's room.

He sat up in bed, rubbing his eyes, his lower lip pouting. She sat and scooped him into her lap and hugged him close.

'Hey, precious. Did you have a bad dream?'

'Yes. It was the bad goblins.' His lip trembled and he tucked his head into her shoulder.

'It's okay now, baby. Mummy's here. I'll slay the silly goblins so they can't get you.'

He gave a sleepy little giggle and wriggled deeper into her embrace.

She sat there, minutes ticking by as she crooned to him, until he fell back asleep. Planting a gentle kiss on his forehead, she caught movement from the corner of her eye and looked up to see Romeo framed in the doorway.

With her emotions nowhere near calm, Maisie couldn't form a coherent thought, never mind form actual words, so she watched in silence as he came and crouched at the side of the bed, his hand trailing gently down Lucca's back.

When his eyes met hers, her breath strangled at the fierce determination brimming in the hazel depths.

'You will slay his imaginary goblins. But what about his real ones?' he murmured, his voice low and intense.

'Romeo—'

'*I* will take care of those. All you have to do is accept my name.'

The implications of what he was asking was no less daunting, no less grave than it'd been half an hour ago when he'd dropped the bombshell. While she'd never given much thought to a future beyond being a mother and owner of a business she loved, she'd also not written it off. But what Romeo was asking… The idea was too huge to even comprehend.

'It's not as monumental an undertaking as you think,' he said, reading her thoughts with an accuracy that terrified her. 'Think of it as a time-buying exercise.'

His gaze fell to Lucca's sleeping form. His hand moved, as if to touch him, but he placed it back down on the bed.

The telling gesture made Maisie's breath strangle in her chest. 'You care about him, don't you?' she murmured.

A look crossed his face, which he quickly blanked. 'I didn't know he existed until twenty-four hours ago. But he's mine, and I take care of what's mine.'

He looked up, the clear, deadly promise blazing for her to see. It shook her to the soul, seeing the promise she'd made to her son the moment he'd drawn breath visible on another person's face.

She opened her mouth to say yes, then felt a cold finger of dread. As much as she wanted to protect her son, she couldn't live with herself if she risked swapping Lucca's physical well-being for his emotional one.

His eyes narrowed, and she was sure he was reading her thoughts again. He gently scooped up Lucca and placed him back in bed, pulling the Lego-themed coverlet over his little body before he straightened.

'Let's finish this talk. Now.' His voice vibrated with low, commanding intensity.

His heavy, dominating presence crowded her as they re-entered the living room. Knowing what she had to say, she turned to face him.

'What's the problem?' he asked.

She threw out her arms. 'Where do you want me to start? Even if I wanted to say yes to what you're proposing, what happens with us?'

A dark frown clamped his forehead. 'Us?'

'Yes, us. You and me. We're virtual strangers. What makes you think we'd last a day under the same roof?'

He shrugged. 'I'm inclined to think if we both know what's at stake, we can make it work.'

And what was at stake was her son's welfare. This was all for Lucca. She was merely the extra passenger along for the ride. The current situation had only made the claiming more urgent. The kiss that had happened was just residual hormones from their last time. Nothing more.

Lucca was the reason Romeo was here in the first place. She didn't think for a second that saying no would send Romeo packing. Regardless of the *Mafia code* or a marriage of convenience, the man in front of her would claim his son. She knew it with a bone-deep certainty.

'Maisie.' Another hard command. She was beginning to recognise how he'd risen to his powerful status so quickly. He packed more imperious presence in his little finger than most men packed in their whole bodies.

'I don't know what to say…'

He waited.

'Before I agree, I need your assurance that you'll resolve this as quickly as possible.'

His nostrils flared, but he nodded. *'Sì.'*

'That you'll tell me if anything changes where protecting Lucca is concerned.'

'You have my word.'

She sucked in a breath, but the enormity of what she was contemplating weighed on her with crushing force. 'Okay… then I'll marry you.'

A golden light flared in his eyes, and he nodded once.

'I'll take care of the details. You don't need to worry about anything.'

With that, he strode to where he'd draped his coat over the sofa and shrugged into it. Surprise scythed through her.

'You're leaving?'

'I have a few phone calls to make. I'll be back in the morning.'

Maisie was still reeling from his words and from what she'd committed herself to hours later when she realised that sleep would remain elusive.

She was still awake at 6:00 a.m. when firm knuckles hammered on her door.

'Is there a particular reason you feel inclined to break down my door at the crack of dawn?'

Romeo raised an eyebrow at the scowl that greeted him from beneath the cloud of auburn hair.

'I would've called, but I didn't want the phone to wake Lucca.' He also hadn't wanted to give her a chance to back out of what he'd convinced her to agree to yesterday.

Nothing would get in the way of him claiming his son. Attempting to give the child who was a part of himself the one thing that was denied him—a chance to choose his own path, free from the stain of illegitimacy.

Romeo might not know or even believe in love. But he could grant Gianlucca the acceptance and security that was never given him.

And Maisie O'Connell wouldn't stand in his way.

But she could, and continued to, glare at him. 'I suppose I should thank you for that consideration.'

'You're not a morning person, I see.'

'Great observation.' She eyed the coffee and croissants in his hand before slicing him with those bright blue eyes again. 'Is one of those for me?' she asked in a gruff, sleep-husky voice.

It was then he noticed the shadows under her eyes. Perhaps he should've waited a little while longer before arriving. But he'd grown tired of pacing his hotel suite. And he hadn't been certain that her *yes* had been from a place of belief that they were doing the right thing. The more he'd paced, the more he'd been sure she would change her mind given any more thinking room.

Romeo intended to give her none.

It had become clear very early on that her devotion to Lucca was absolute. It had been the only thing that had made him leave last night.

That and the need to push his investigators harder to find something concrete he could use against Lorenzo.

'Is that a no?'

He focused to see Maisie sliding a hairband from her wrist. She caught it in her teeth, then gathered her heavy silky hair into a bunch at the back of her head. The action drew up her nightshirt, showing off her shapely thighs and legs. Heat trickled through him as his gaze trailed up to linger on her heavy, pert breasts, thrown into relief by the act of securing her hair.

She seemed to notice the thick layer of awareness that had fired up, and her eyes darkened a touch.

Reining in his libido and burying the recollection of how those breasts had felt in his hands last night, he held out the coffee. There would be no repeat of last night's lust-fuelled encounter. Romeo had no intention of letting sex clutter up his plans.

He of all people knew one moment of madness could destroy a life. It was the reason he existed. It was the reason his mother had spent years blaming him for destroying her life.

It's the reason your son's here.

He accepted that sound analysis, just as he'd accepted that now he knew of Lucca's existence, he would safeguard his upbringing with everything he possessed. He'd witnessed too many people fall through the cracks to leave his son's fate to miracles and chance.

His own existence had been proof that miracles didn't exist.

'Thank you,' Maisie murmured huskily, taking the proffered beverage before stepping back to let him in. He handed her the pastry and followed her into the kitchen. She placed the croissants on a plate but didn't make a move to touch them. 'It's a little too early for me.'

Again he experienced a tiny bout of guilt, then told himself there would be plenty of time for her to rest once he got them away from here.

Her gaze flicked to him, then darted away. But in that look Romeo caught the hesitation he'd been dreading. He gritted his teeth.

He didn't want to resort to plan B, but he would if necessary. 'Second thoughts are natural. As long as you keep your eye on the big picture.'

She bit her lip. 'I can't believe this is happening.'

'It's happening, *gattina*. We'll tell Lucca when he wakes up. Is there anyone else you wish to inform? Your parents?' He vaguely recalled her mentioning them in the intermittent burst of chatter that had preceded him inviting her to his suite that night in Palermo.

Her expression shuttered and she took a large gulp of coffee. 'My parents are no longer in the picture.' A bleak note of hurt threaded her voice. 'And even if they were, this wouldn't be the ideal scenario to present to them, would it? Their only child marrying the father of her child because the Mafia were issuing threats?' Her mouth twisted in mocking bitterness.

His eyes narrowed at the odd note in her voice. 'They wouldn't want you to do what is necessary to safeguard their grandson?'

Her gaze remained lowered and she crossed her arms around her middle in a gesture of self-preservation. 'I wouldn't know. Besides the odd birthday and Christmas card, I haven't spoken to them in four years.'

Four years. The same length of time as his son had been alive. Certain there was more to the story, he opened his mouth to ask. But her head snapped up and she flashed him a pursed-lip smile.

'How much time do I have to get my things in order? I'll need a few days at least to talk to... You're shaking your head. Why?' she enquired curtly.

'We're leaving this morning.'

'That's impossible. I have to pack and make sure I get the right person to look after the restaurant until...' She stopped and frowned. 'Will I be able to return any time soon?' Wide blue eyes stared at him with a mixture of resignation and sadness.

'Not for a while.'

'How long is a while?'

'A few weeks, a few months? It's probably best that you forget about this place for the time being.'

The sadness was replaced with a flash of anger. 'That's easy for you to say. You haven't spent the better part of two years working night and day to get a business off the ground.'

He allowed himself a small smile. 'I know a little bit about the hard work it takes to establish a business.'

She grimaced. 'But you don't know how it feels to do it on your own with no support from anyone else. The fear that comes from knowing that one failure could mean you have nothing to help you look after your child.' She shook her head, as if realising how much she'd revealed.

Romeo chose not to enlighten her about his personal relationship with fear and failure—of the rough, terrifying nights he'd spent on the streets when he was barely into his teens; of the desperate need for acceptance that had led him to contemplate, for a blessedly brief moment, whether he was truly his father's son.

He'd rejected and stumbled away from the gang initiation rites and earned himself a bullseye on his back for a while. But it hadn't stopped the fermenting thought that perhaps the life of a *Mafioso* was blueprinted in his blood.

That was a part of him he intended would never see the light of day.

But it was a thought he had never been able to shake off.

He downed the espresso and watched her struggle to get her emotions under control. 'Tell me what you need to do to expedite things.' He had spent most of the night putting things in place to remove her and Lucca as quickly as possible, but he had the feeling telling her that right now wouldn't go down well.

'I have to speak to Bronagh about assuming a full-time managerial position for starters. Then make sure the staff are taken care of.' She started to slide her hands through her hair, realised she'd caught it in a ponytail and switched to sliding the long tail through her fingers. 'I can't just up and leave.'

The need to get her and Lucca away from here, as quickly as possible, smashed through the civilised barrier he'd placed on himself so far. 'A Michelin-star chef will be here at nine to take over the day-to-day running of the restaurant. Once Lucca is awake, I have a team of movers waiting outside to pack your things. You can keep the apartment or I can arrange for it to be sold, that's your choice. We'll stop over in London, where we will be married at four this afternoon. After that we'll fly straight from London to my island in Hawaii.'

She'd stilled as he spoke, her eyes growing wider with each plan he laid out. 'But...we can't get married that quickly,' she blurted. 'We need a special licence and that takes—'

'It's taken care of.'

She shook her head. 'This is going too fast, Romeo.'

He folded his arms. 'The sooner this layer of protection

is in place, the sooner I can concentrate on dealing with Lorenzo.'

Apprehension crept into her eyes and he cursed under his breath.

She abandoned her coffee and folded her arms. Romeo willed his gaze to remain above her neckline, not to watch the tail of hair trail across her breasts with each breath she took. 'Do we at least have time to discuss what sort of marriage we're going to have?'

He tensed. 'Excuse me?'

'Well, this isn't going to be a traditional marriage, is it? As you said, we're only doing this to ensure Lucca's safety, so I presume the physical side of things won't be part of the marriage.'

Despite having told himself precisely the same thing after his control slipped last night, something moved through his belly that felt very much like rejection. He gritted his teeth.

'If that is what you wish, then it will be so.'

Her lashes swept down. 'Yes, that's what I want. I think you'll agree, sex tends to cause unnecessary confusion.' A flush crept up her neck and Romeo was struck by how innocent she looked.

'*Sì*, Lucca is the most important thing in all this.' Why did the words feel so hard to get out?

She gave a brisk nod. 'I'll go and get changed. He'll be waking up any minute now.' She started to walk towards the door, then stopped and turned with a grace that hinted at balletic training.

Romeo frowned. He knew next to nothing about the mother of his child. All he had were the basic facts produced by his private investigators. He'd been so focused on his son that he'd only requested information from Maisie's pregnancy to date.

He hadn't really paid attention to their random conversations five years ago. He'd gone seeking oblivion of the carnal nature and had fallen head first into a maelstrom of emotions he still had a hard time reliving. He'd tried afterwards to explain it away as his grief talking, but that hadn't quite rung true.

The idea that he'd been burying a lonely yearning that had chosen his mother's death to emerge had shaken him to the core.

It wasn't a place he wanted to visit ever again.

He mentally shrugged. He didn't *need* to know any more about Maisie, other than that she would continue to remain devoted and invested in keeping their son safe.

'I'd like to keep Bronagh as assistant manager. She's been a huge support and I don't want this new manager tossing her out after I'm gone, okay?'

'If that's what you need to put your mind at rest, then it will be done.'

She opened her mouth, as if she wanted to say more, but nodded and left.

His phone vibrated in his pocket. He pulled it out before it started to ring. Anger throbbed to life when he saw the familiar area code. Strolling out of the kitchen, he answered it.

'You may be used to not taking no for an answer, but if you want to have any dealings with me, you'll listen when I say I'll be in touch when I'm good and ready.'

'You have the benefit of youth on your side, Brunetti, but I'm reduced to counting the minutes.'

'Perhaps you should remember that before you test me any further,' he grated out.

Lorenzo gave a barking laugh. 'You think I don't know what you're up to? You may secure your *figlio* a layer of protection, but your legacy will still need to be claimed.'

Romeo's rage built. 'My legacy doesn't involve indulging a handful of geriatric old men, desperate to hang on to the old ways. I'm better at this game than you give me credit for. Being forced to live in the gutter has a way of bringing out a man's survival instincts.'

For the first time, Lorenzo seemed to falter. 'Brunetti…'

'Do not call me again. I'll be in touch when I'm ready.'
He hung up and turned at the sound of his son's laughter.

The sound moved through him, and he froze in place for a second.

Gianlucca was his legacy. One he intended to guard with his life, if necessary.

He swallowed and got himself under control just as his son burst excitedly into the living room.

'Mummy says we're going on a plane today!'

'Yes, you're coming to live with me for a little while.'

'Do you have a big house?'

The corner of Romeo's mouth lifted. 'It's big enough for my needs, yes.'

Lucca's head tilted pensively. 'Does it have a duck pond?'

'Not yet,' he replied, then gave in to the compulsion to offer more; to make a little boy happy. 'But I will build one for you.'

His eyes rounded. 'My very own duck pond?' he whispered in awe.

A peculiar stone lodged in Romeo's throat, making it difficult to swallow. '*Sì*…yes. Your very own.'

A giant smile broke over his son's face. 'Wow! Can I also have a bouncy castle?'

Romeo opened his mouth, but Maisie shook her head. 'We'll discuss it later.'

Lucca continued to beam. 'It's going to be the best adventure ever!'

Unable to speak on account of all the tectonic plates of his reality shifting inside him, Romeo could only nod.

CHAPTER SIX

MAISIE FOUND OUT just how much of an adventure when she was ushered into an exclusive Mayfair boutique five hours later with a team of stylists. As per Romeo's imperious request, the shop had been shut so the attendants could focus solely on her. He sat in the large reception room, flipping through a document while keeping an eye on Lucca, who was getting his own special outfit for the wedding.

Wedding...

She was getting married. To the father of her child. The man she'd thought she'd never set eyes on again after waking up alone in a hotel room in Palermo. The dizzying turn of events threatened to flatten her. But as she'd taken to reminding herself in case any fanciful thoughts took over, all this was happening for the sake of her son.

This was a wedding in name only; it would *be* a marriage in name only. And once this whole business with Romeo's dark past was over with, she would resume her life.

All the same, she couldn't stop a bewildering shiver as the wedding dress she'd chosen was slipped over her head.

Made entirely of cream silk, the calf-length dress had the scoop-neck design both in the front and back, and lace sleeves covering her to the elbow. The material hugged her from bodice to thigh, with a slit at the back for ease of movement. It was simple, elegant and businesslike enough to not portray any of those fanciful thoughts that fleeted through her mind every time she so much as dropped her guard. Dress on, she slipped her feet into matching cream heels and moved to where a hair and make-up expert had been set up.

Maisie had lost the ability to keep up with how fast Romeo had moved once things were set in motion. There'd been no time to get sentimental once she'd summoned the staff, especially with Romeo's overwhelming presence at her side reassuring them that nothing would change in the running of the restaurant.

Her staff knew and respected Bronagh. It was that alone that had made temporarily stepping away from the place she'd poured her heart and muscle into bearable.

And then Romeo had floored her by inviting Bronagh to London to act as witness at their wedding.

The surprises had kept coming, with her first, brief trip in a private jet, hammering home to her just how powerful and influential the man she would be marrying shortly really was.

'There, I think you're set.'

Maisie refocused and examined the chic pinned-up hairstyle and subtle, immaculate make-up, and forced a smile. As much as she'd told herself this marriage wasn't real, she couldn't halt the horde of butterflies beating frantically in her belly. 'Thank you.'

'And I hope you don't mind, but we sent out for a bouquet. It seems a little wrong that a bride should get married without one, you know?' The owner of the boutique, an elegant, fortyish woman, said. 'Especially when you're marrying Romeo Brunetti.' The clear envy in her eyes and the awe in her voice echoed through Maisie.

She was saved from answering when the door opened and Bronagh entered holding a stunning cream-and-lilac rose arrangement bound with crystal-studded ribbon. 'I'd say this bouquet is the most gorgeous thing I've ever seen, but I think you take the prize for that, Maisie,' she said, her soft brown eyes widening as Maisie rose and she looked her over. 'You're going to knock that man of yours dead.' There was a faintly querying note in her voice, but the reason Maisie had become fast friends with Bronagh Davis was because she'd offered friendship without prying just when Maisie had needed that. And although the other woman had probably guessed that Romeo was Lucca's father—the similarities between them seemed to grow with each passing second—she hadn't questioned Maisie.

'You win all the points for flattery,' Maisie replied, surreptitiously rubbing her palms together to keep them from getting any more damp.

Bronagh smiled and handed over the bouquet. 'You can award me the points later. Your men are getting impatient, and from the way the older one is pacing, I wouldn't be surprised if he storms in here and claims you.'

The butterflies' wings flapped harder. Maisie swallowed down her absurd nervousness and any lingering sadness that indicated she wished this were real, that she were marrying a man she'd taken the time to meet, fall in love and ultimately join her life with.

That was a pipe dream she'd long ago abandoned, even before she'd been faced with an unplanned pregnancy and the sheer dedication she'd needed to take care of her child. She'd been exposed too many times to the ruthless indifference inherent in loveless relationships to believe that she would be the exception to the rule. The love she'd felt for Lucca the moment he was born had been a miraculous gift she intended to guard with everything she held dear. So she'd driven her energy into providing a home for her child, despite her parents' icy disapproval.

Maisie reminded herself that this situation wasn't in her control, that even in this she was putting Lucca's needs first.

Her needs didn't matter.

That particular thought took a steep dive when she emerged from the changing room and was confronted with Romeo Brunetti in a three-piece suit. Immaculate, imposingly masculine and utterly breathtaking, he was impossible to ignore. From the top of his neatly combed, wavy black hair, to the polished toes of his handmade shoes, he reeked irrefutable power and enough sexual magnetism to make kings quake and women swoon in his presence. And that look in his eyes…that brooding, almost formidable intensity that had made her tingle from head to toe the first time she'd seen him…

Yes. Maisie was reminded then how very needful she could be. And how some needs were impossible to suppress even with an iron will. She stared. Tried to pull her gaze away. Failed. And stared some more. At the back of her mind, a tiny voice said it was okay to stare because he was doing the same to her.

The look in his eyes was riveting, as if he were seeing her for the first time. A part of her thrilled at that look, the way it made her feel sexy and desirable…until she reminded herself that nothing would come of it. Nothing could.

Her attention was mercifully pulled away when Lucca rushed towards her. 'You look beautiful, Mummy!'

Her smile wobbled when she saw his own attire—a miniature one of his father's, right down to the buttoned-up waistcoat. 'So do you, my precious.'

Romeo seemed to unfreeze then from his stance. 'Come, the car's waiting.'

Everyone snapped to attention. Two guards appeared at the shop door and nodded. They exited and slid into the back of the limo and were driving the short distance to the register office at Marylebone when he reached into his jacket, pulled out a long, velvet box and handed it to her.

'What's this?' she blurted.

One corner of his mouth lifted. 'I thought your absence of jewellery should be addressed.'

Her hand went to her bare throat. 'I…I didn't think it was necessary.' Which, in hindsight, sounded a little foolish. She was marrying one of the world's richest men. Whether the marriage was real or not, she was about to be thrust into the limelight the proportions of which she was too afraid to imagine. The women Romeo had dated before were all raving beauties compared to her.

A flush rose in her face when his eyebrow quirked. 'You may not, but we don't wish to attract unnecessary gossip,' he murmured, his voice deep but low enough to keep Bronagh and Lucca, who sat on the far side of the limo, from overhearing. 'Open it.'

Fingers shaking, she prised the box open and gasped. The three-layered collar necklace contained over two dozen diamonds in different cuts and sizes, the largest, teardrop gem placed in the middle. The stunning jewels, along with a pair of equally breathtaking earrings, sparkled in her trembling hand. Maisie realised her mouth was still open when Romeo plucked the necklace off its velvet bed and held it out.

'Turn around.'

Still stunned, she complied and suppressed a tremble when his warm fingers brushed her nape. She turned towards him to thank him and froze when he leaned forward to adjust the necklace so the large stone was resting just above her cleavage. The touch of those fingers…there… sent her blood pounding through her veins. She looked up and met dark hazel eyes. The knowing and hungry look reflecting back at her stopped whatever breath she'd been about to take. They stared at each other, that intense connection that seemed to fuse them together whenever they were close sizzling between them.

'Wow, that's stunning.'

Maisie jerked guiltily at Bronagh's awed compliment. Another blush crept into her face when she realised she'd momentarily forgotten that her friend and son were in the car. To cover up her embarrassment, she hastily reached for the earrings and clipped them on. Then exhaled in a rush when Romeo produced another ominous-sized box.

'Romeo…'

His eyes flashed a warning and she swallowed her objection. This time he opened it. The large diamond-and-ruby engagement ring defied description. And probably defied any attempt to place a value on it. Silently, Maisie held out her left hand, absurdly bemused to take in the fact that between one heartbeat and the next she'd been draped in jewels that cost more than she would earn in a lifetime.

She smiled through further gasps from Bronagh and just willed herself to breathe. She might not have fully absorbed what she was letting herself in for publicly by agreeing to marry Romeo Brunetti the billionaire, instead of Romeo Brunetti, father of her child, but she'd faced tougher challenges and triumphed. She could do this.

The marriage ceremony itself was shockingly brief.

Whatever strings Romeo had pulled to secure a special licence had pressed home his importance. They were ushered into an oak-panelled room that reeked history and brevity. The registrar read out their commitments in a deep but hushed voice and announced that they were man and wife within twenty minutes of their arrival.

Romeo's kiss on her lips was swift and chaste, his hands dropping from her shoulders almost immediately. She told herself the wrench in her stomach was nerves as she followed him to the desk where their signatures formalised their union.

As she signed her name, Maisie reaffirmed that she was taking the necessary steps to keep her son safe. It was what kept her going through the lavish Mayfair meal with Bronagh, after which Bronagh was driven to the airport to catch a flight back to Dublin, and they were driven straight to a private airport south of London.

Unable to stand the thick silence in the car now that Lucca had fallen asleep, she cleared her throat.

'I didn't know Italians could marry in London without jumping through bureaucratic hoops.'

Romeo switched from looking out of the window. The brooding glance he sent her made her wish for a moment she'd let the silence continue. 'I've lived in London for over ten years. Other than two days ago, the last time I was in Italy was when you and I met.'

Surprise lifted her brows. 'I thought you were a resident. You seemed to know your way about where...where you were staying.'

His mouth twisted. 'I was, once upon a time. But in a much more inhospitable part.'

'Inhospitable?' she echoed.

That brooding gaze intensified. 'I wasn't always affluent, *gattina*. I can probably go as far as to say I'm the definition of *nouveau riche*. I know the streets where we met well because I used to walk there at night in the hope that I would find leftover food in bins or a tourist who was willing to part with a few euros for a quick shoe shine. Barring that, I would find an alleyway to sleep in for a night, but only for a night because inevitably I would be sent packing by the *polizia* and threatened with jail should I return.'

Maisie wasn't sure which was more unnerving—the harrowing account of his childhood or the cold, unfeeling way in which he recounted it. Either way, the stone-cold horror that had wedged in her stomach grew, until she was sure her insides were frozen with pain at imagining what he'd been through.

'You said you only met your father twice,' she murmured, unable to erase the bleak picture he drew in her mind, 'but what about your mother?'

Lucca stirred in his sleep, and Romeo's eyes shifted to his son before returning to hers. 'My mother is a subject I don't wish to discuss, especially on my wedding day.' His smile mocked the significance of the day.

But Maisie couldn't dismiss the subject as easily. 'And child services? Surely there was some support you could've sought?'

He blinked, his nostrils flaring slightly before he shrugged. 'The support is the same in Italy as it is in England. Some fall through the cracks. And if one tried hard enough to evade the clutches of a system that was inherently flawed, one could succeed.'

Despite catching his meaning, Maisie couldn't fathom why he would choose to live on the streets. 'How long did you sleep rough for?' she asked, her heart bleeding at the thought.

His mouth compressed in a cruel line. 'Two years until the authorities got fed up with hauling me away every other night. A do-gooder policewoman thought I would be better off in the foster system.' He gave a harsh, self-deprecating laugh. 'Unfortunately, she couldn't have been more wrong. Because then it was really driven home that my kind wouldn't be welcome in a normal, well-adjusted home.'

'Your kind?'

'The bastard children of violent criminals.'

Her hand flew to her mouth. 'Oh, God!'

Romeo's eyes once again flicked to his sleeping son and he shook his head. 'Don't worry, *gattina*. I got out the second I could. Now look at me.' He spread his hands in mock preen. And although his voice was even, Maisie saw the shadows of dark memory that blanketed his eyes and hardened his mouth. 'According to the media, I'm every woman's dream and every parent's ideal suitor for their wholesome daughter. Consider yourself lucky for bagging me.' His teeth barred in a mirthless smile.

'Romeo—'

He lunged close so quickly, filled every inch of her vision so spectacularly, her breath snagged in her chest. His fingers pressed against her mouth, forcibly rejecting any words she'd been about to utter. 'No, *gattina*. Save your warm-hearted sympathy and soft words for our son,' he rasped jaggedly. 'You be there for him when he scrapes his knee and when the goblins frighten him at night. I require no sympathy. I learnt to do without it long before I could walk.'

He sat back and for a full minute remained frozen. Then

his chest rose and fell in a single deep exhalation before he pressed a button next to his armrest. A laptop slid from a side compartment and flickered on. Strong fingers tapped the keys, flicking through pages of data with calm efficiency.

As if he hadn't just torn open his chest and shown her the raw wounds scarring his heart.

Romeo tapped another random key, stared unseeing at the stream of words and numbers filling the screen.

What in the name of heaven had he been thinking?

Had he not sworn only last night to keep his past locked in the vault where it belonged? Through all the voracious media attention that had exploded in his life once his first resort had achieved platinum-star status, he'd kept his past safely under wraps. Besides Zaccheo Giordano, the only man he considered a friend, and his wife, Eva, no one else knew about the desperately traumatising childhood he'd suffered. Many had tried to dig, only to accept the illusion that his secret past made him alluringly mysterious, and left it at that. Romeo had been more than glad to leave things at that.

So why had he just spilled his guts to Maisie O'Connell? And not only spilled his guts, but ripped off the emotion-free bandage he'd bound his memories with in the process?

He tried to think through it rationally; to decipher just what it was about this woman who let all the volatile, raw emotions overrun him.

Their meeting hadn't been accompanied by thunder and lightning. There'd been nothing remotely spectacular about it. To the contrary, he'd walked past her that night at the waterfront café in Palermo with every intention of continuing his solitary walk.

Lost in thoughts of bewildering grief and hoping the night air would clear his head, he'd walked for miles from the cemetery where Ariana Brunetti had found her last resting place. He'd barely taken in where he was headed, the

need to put distance between the mother whose only interest had been for herself and how much she could get for
selling her body, a visceral need.

When he'd finally reached the stone wall overlooking
the water, he'd stood lost and seriously contemplated scal-
ing the wall and swimming away from the city that bore
only harrowing memories. The sound of tourists drinking
away the night had finally impinged, and he'd had the brilliant idea of drowning his sorrows with whisky.

He'd walked past her, barely noticing her.

It was only as he'd ordered his third whisky that he'd
caught her staring. Even then, he'd dismissed her. He was
used to women staring at him. Women coming onto him
since he'd been old enough to shave.

But he'd caught her furtive glances, those bright blue
eyes darting his way when she thought he wasn't looking.
Romeo wasn't sure why he'd talked to her that night. Perhaps it'd been that lost look she'd been trying so hard to disguise. Or the fact that a group of male tourists had noticed
her and were placing bets on who would buy her the next
drink. Or the fact that his mother's last words to him had
left him raw, feeling as if his very skin had been peeled off.

You're just like him...just like him...

In the hours and days that had followed, he'd been able
to stop those words ringing in his head.

Having that drink in that café had been a last, desperate
attempt to drown out the words.

He'd raised his glass to her in a silent toast. She'd smiled
shyly and asked what he was toasting. He'd made some
smart remark or other he couldn't recall. He'd kicked out
the seat opposite in brusque invitation and she'd joined him.

Midnight had arrived and they'd walked to his hotel,
both of them very much aware of what would happen next.

He'd walked away the next day, even more exposed than
he'd ever been in his life.

But he'd pulled himself together, refusing to be the needy

shadow of a man who'd yearned for a kind word from the mother who'd rejected him all his life. And he'd succeeded.

Nothing should've prompted this puzzling and clever way Maisie had managed to slip under his guard not once, but twice. It was a weakness he couldn't, *wouldn't* abide.

He stole a glance from the corner of his eye and saw that she was gazing at the passing scenery, her fingers toying with her new rings.

He breathed a little easier, confident that moment of madness was behind him. That she was taking his advice and letting the temporary aberration pass.

'I'm sorry I dredged up bad memories for you,' she said suddenly.

Romeo shut the laptop with studied care, resisting the urge to rip the gadget out of its housing and throw it out of the window.

'Maisie—' he growled warningly.

'I know you don't want to talk about it now and I respect that. But I just wanted you to know, should you ever feel the need to talk, I'm here.'

For one shocking, ground-shaking moment, his black soul lifted at those words. He allowed himself to glimpse a day when he would unburden himself and feel whole, clean. The picture was so laughable, he shook his head in wonder at his own gall.

He was the son of a whore and a vicious thug. He'd contemplated hurting another human being just so he could join a gang…to gain respect through violence. Walking away, sick to his stomach, hadn't absolved him of the three days he'd worn the probation leathers and trawled the dark streets of Palermo, looking for a victim. He would never be clean, never be washed free of that stain. He hadn't bothered to try up until now. He never would.

'*Grazie*, but I can assure you that day will never come.'

CHAPTER SEVEN

THE BRUNETTI INTERNATIONAL RESORT MAUI was a tropical oasis that had been created with heaven itself in mind. Or at least that was what the brochure stated.

Maisie had silently rolled her eyes when she read the claim.

Looking around her as they alighted from the seaplane, she accepted the statement hadn't been an exaggeration. A long, sugar-sanded beach stretched for a half mile before it curved around an outcrop of rock that looked perfect for diving.

From the beach, the land rose gently, swaying palm trees blending with the increasingly denser vegetation Maisie had spotted from the plane before they'd landed.

She knew the resort housed six koa-wood-and-stone mansions, each large and luxurious enough to cater to the most demanding guest, with the largest, a twelve-bedroom sprawling architect's dream, sitting on top of a hill in the centre of the island.

From the brochure she'd read she also knew that the mansion had been booked for the next three years and that guests paid a king's ransom for the privilege.

She had been admiring the stunning architecture of the resort when her eyes had grown heavy. Jerking awake, she'd found her shoes had been taken off, her seat reclined and a pillow tucked under her head. She'd looked up from the soft cashmere throw keeping her warm to find Lucca and Romeo at the dining table, tucking into a meal. Or rather, Lucca had been eating and chattering away, with his father watching him with that silent intensity and awe that had struck a peculiar ache in Maisie's chest.

Romeo had looked up then, locked gazes with her before being diverted by their son. Unlike in the car when his emotions had bubbled just beneath his skin, he'd looked cool and remote, very much the powerful, in-control billionaire. He'd looked untouchable, and Maisie believed he meant for the moment in the car never to happen again. Whatever had prompted him to reveal a horrific chapter of his past had been resealed in an impenetrable fortress, never to be revisited again.

She'd berated herself for feeling mournful, for experiencing his pain as acutely as if it were her own. She had no right to it, no right to pry or feel strangely bereft when he'd shut her out and refocused his attention on Lucca.

Her parents had tried to drill into her that her brain was her most valuable asset, but Maisie had known that wasn't true. With the birth of her child, she'd known love was the greatest gift she could give, and receive. Same as she knew that Romeo, like her parents, didn't have a need for it. He believed in protecting his son, much as her own parents had provided a roof over her head and put clothes on her back. But, like them, he had nothing more to give.

And while she couldn't turn her compassion off at will, she needed to guard against overexposure of the emotion that had drawn her to Romeo in the first place. His grief and misery that night had been like a beacon. She'd wanted to comfort him, grant him reprieve from the shackles that bound him.

The result had been waking up alone, and returning home weeks later, pregnant. She would do well to remember that.

'Are you coming?'

She jumped at Romeo's prompt and realised she'd stopped at the bottom of the stone steps leading up from the beach.

'Yes, of course.' She smiled at the six white-uniformed staff ready to unload their luggage and followed Romeo up to the buggy parked on the pavement. He lowered an excited Lucca onto the seat and fastened his seat belt before turning to her.

'Would you like a quick tour now or later?' he asked coolly.

'Now would be great, thanks.'

He nodded and started the buggy. When Lucca wriggled excitedly, Romeo slowed down and touched his son's arm. 'Sit still, *bambino*, or you'll have to walk all the way back to the house.'

Lucca looked round. 'Where's the house?' he asked.

Romeo pointed up the hill to a large villa whose glass cathedral-like dome dominated the hilltop. 'All the way up there.'

Lucca immediately stilled, his eyes rounding as he stared up at Romeo. 'I'll be still.'

Romeo looked over at her, a small smile playing on his lips before he tentatively ruffled Lucca's hair. '*Bene*…that means good in Italian.'

'*Bene,*' Lucca repeated, intoning the syllables in near perfect match of his father's accent.

Maisie looked around and realised two things. That the brochure hadn't done enough justice to the description of Hana Island. And also that only two of the mansions that Romeo drove past looked occupied.

'But I thought this place was fully booked for years in advance?'

'It was…until yesterday when I cancelled half of the bookings.'

'Why?'

'Because I wanted to guarantee our privacy. The two families who are staying here have been fully vetted and have signed confidentiality agreements. The others were a little more testy, so I compensated them for their trouble and sent them to another resort. Complimentary, of course.'

Maisie looked around as they headed up the hill. The whole place was the very epitome of paradise. But then paradise had contained a poisonous snake.

'Surely you don't think...'

He sent her a warning look. She bit her lip and waited until he'd stopped the buggy in front of a large set of double doors made of polished koa wood and released Lucca's seat belt. When Lucca scampered off towards the house, he turned to her.

'No, I don't think we'll have any trouble here, but I took the necessary precautions nevertheless.'

She looked around the lush paradise. 'But we can't stay here for ever, Romeo.'

His jaw flexed. 'We'll remain here until I find a way to fix this. Besides, the world thinks we're on our honeymoon, so why not enjoy the time off?' He glanced over to where Lucca was examining a spray of giant bright orange flowers. 'I can't imagine you've had any downtime since he was born.'

Maisie smiled reluctantly. 'I don't imagine I'll be getting any until he's at least eighteen.'

He watched her with a quizzical look. 'But it will be a relief not to be burdened with him 24/7, *sì*?' There was a hard bite to his tone that set her nerves on edge.

She frowned. 'I don't consider him a burden,' she retorted.

'Was he the reason you switched careers?' he enquired.

'Well...yes, but—'

'Pursuing a career in criminal law to operating a restaurant in a quaint little village is quite a change.'

'It was a choice I made both for Lucca and myself.'

He nodded. 'You've proved you're capable of adapting. So adjusting to our new situation shouldn't be a big problem.'

She looked around. 'I'm not built to lie about sipping cocktails. I need a challenge, even with Lucca around.'

'Then we will find other challenges for you.'

'Thank you. Now, is this interview of my mothering skills and commitment over? I'd like to get out of these travelling clothes.'

He continued to stare at her in that direct, invasive way of his, as if trying to see beneath her words to any truth she was hiding.

After several minutes he nodded and alighted from the buggy.

Double doors swung open and two women came forward, one an older Tongan native and a younger girl who approached Lucca with a smile. Maisie noticed she walked with a slight limp.

'This is Emily. She'll be helping you look after Lucca. And Mahina is our housekeeper.'

Maisie managed to keep a smile on her face throughout the introductions and the tour of Romeo's mansion. She even managed to make the right noises when she saw the Olympic-sized pool and the hot tub, and the man-made cave that opened up into a private waterfall complete with pool at the back of the property.

She smiled through giving Lucca a quick wash, with a helpful Emily unpacking his clothes. When the girl offered to take him away for a glass of juice, Maisie forced a nod, welcoming the opportunity to find Romeo and give him a piece of her mind.

After searching fruitlessly upstairs and knocking on over a dozen doors, she finally found him in a large, airy room converted to a study, with rows of books covering one wall, and an imposing desk and chair fronting a floor-to-ceiling glass window.

She shut the door behind her after his imperious directive to come in and stalked to where he sat, master and commander of his empire.

'How dare you hire a nanny without consulting me,' she fired at him when he looked up from the document he was perusing.

His brows clamped for a second before he rose and rounded the desk. Maisie forced herself not to step back from the broad-shouldered magnificence of his physique. He'd also changed from the suit he wore to travel, into a turquoise polo shirt and a pair of white linen trousers, into which he shoved his hands. 'I didn't think you would object.'

'Why? Because I'm so eager to be lightened of the *burden* of caring for my son?'

'Because I'm told every mother needs a break every now and then.'

'And who, pray tell, enlightened you of this fact? It can't have been your mother, since I'm guessing she wasn't a contender for mother of the year?'

His cold tensing confirmed she'd gone too far. 'We seem to be straying away from the issue under discussion. You slept for less than an hour on the plane and I'm sure you didn't have much sleep the night before. The jet lag will kick in very hard shortly.' He shrugged. 'I thought you would welcome the help.'

She told herself not to soften at his consideration. 'Is that all she is—temporary help?' she pressed.

'No. She helps around the resort when needed, but she's the only one with childcare training.'

She shook her head. 'Romeo—'

Narrowed eyes studied her closely. 'What exactly is the problem here?'

'The problem is you made a decision about Lucca's care without consulting me.'

He exhaled with a rush of irritation. 'This is an adjustment for all of us, Lucca included. Some decisions will have to be made with or without your input.'

'No, I don't accept that. Not when it comes to my son.'

He shrugged. 'Okay, you can use Emily when you see

fit, or not at all. I'll leave that decision up to you. But you can't control every moment of his life, Maisie.'

Cold anger robbed her of breath for a moment. Then the words came tumbling out. 'You've known him for what, two days? And you dare to say that to me?'

His eyes turned a burnished gold. 'Is it my fault that I didn't know of his existence before then?'

'Well, it's not mine! Had you bothered to stick around the morning after—'

'For what purpose? Exchange false promises of hooking up again? Or perhaps you wanted compliments on what a great night we shared?'

An angry flush replaced the cold rage. 'I don't know why you're being so vile! And pardon me if I didn't know the right etiquette for the morning after one-night stands. That was my first and last experience. But I certainly didn't think I'd wake up alone with no trace of the man I'd spent the night with. Or that you'd instruct the concierge not to divulge any information as to your identity. If you want to be angry at anyone, be angry at yourself, because despite that deplorable behaviour, despite you leaving me there to do the walk of shame on my own, I still went back to look for you when I found out I was pregnant.'

His face froze in a mask of surprise. 'You did what?'

'I went back. I used savings I would've been better off investing for my unborn child to pay for a two-week stay in that exorbitant hotel. I walked the streets of Palermo every day and visited every café I could find for a fortnight.' She laughed. 'I drank enough decaf lattes to float a cruise ship, all in the hope that I might find you. Do you know how many hits there are for *Romeo of Palermo* on the Internet?'

He shook his head slowly, as if in a daze.

'Well, I won't bore you with figures. Let's just say tracking every one of them down would've taken me years. I didn't speak the language, so either I was laughed off or every enquiry was met with a blank look. So, yes, I gave up after two weeks and decided my time would be better spent planning a safe and comfortable future for my son. So don't you dare tell me I won't be consulted about each and every decision where he's concerned. And don't you dare make me feel bad about the consequences of something that we both did *consensually*.'

A red flush scoured his cheekbones before he inhaled deeply. Whirling about, he strode to the window and gazed out at the spectacular view.

When she was convinced the silence would stretch for ever, she approached and stood next to him. 'Are you going to say something?' she ventured in a quieter voice once several more minutes had passed.

He slanted a glance at her. 'It is not often I'm surprised. But you have surprised me, *gattina*,' he rasped.

'Because I've shown that underneath that auburn hair I have a temper?' she half joked.

A flicker of a smile ghosted over his lips. 'That wasn't a surprise. I'm very much aware of the depths of your passion.'

She reddened and glanced away before she was tempted to read a different meaning to his words. 'What, then?'

'What you did…' He paused and shook his head. 'No other person I know would've done that. And you're right. After the way I left, you had every right to write me off. And I did make sure that I would not be easy to find.'

'That's an understatement. Do you do that often? Erase your presence so thoroughly your conquests can never find you?' she asked before she could stop herself.

'Not in such direct terms. There is usually an understanding of the transient nature of my liaisons.'

'Oh…right.' That told her.

'That night was different for me, too, in many ways.'

She wanted to ask, but that bleak, haunted look was back in his eyes again, along with that do-not-disturb force field that told her she would risk emotional electrocution if she so much as raised an eyebrow in inquiry. To her surprise, he continued.

'It had been a trying day, one I didn't wish to face even though I knew it was coming.'

'Yeah, we all have days like that.'

He looked at her, his gaze brushing her face, her throat, her body, before turning his attention to the window again. 'But you came back, despite feeling the sting of rejection and perhaps a lot aggrieved?' he asked.

'I put myself in my child's shoes and knew that I needed to give him a chance to know his father. But I guess a part of me was terrified that I couldn't do this on my own and was in some way looking for support.' She shrugged. 'The moment I got back to Dublin, I accepted that I was in this alone. Then Lucca was born, and with each day that passed the fear receded. I was no longer alone. I had him.'

His stare returned, stayed longer this time. 'You're no longer alone where his care is concerned.'

She raised her eyebrows. 'But you don't agree that I should be consulted on all things?'

A steely look entered his eyes. 'I'll grant you a healthy debate about the major issues that concern him. And you can attempt to tear me to pieces on the minor ones.'

'So in other words, we'll argue about everything?'

The corner of his mouth lifted. 'Only because you seem to thrive on arguments.'

Her mouth curved in answer. 'Be warned, I never stop until I get my way.'

His eyes dropped to her mouth, and a heated channel forged between them. Her breath shallowed, her heart racing as she read the look loud and clear.

Desire thickened in her veins, her core throbbing until she yearned to squeeze her thighs together to alleviate the ache.

'Perhaps I will let you win on occasion,' he murmured,

his voice husky and deep. When his gaze dropped to linger on her breasts, a light tremble went through her.

She was thinking it was wise to move away before she did something foolish, like rise on tiptoe and taste his mouth, when a knock sounded on the door.

'Yes?' he answered, his eyes still on her.

Emily entered with Lucca, who smiled broadly when he saw her. 'Lucca wants to go for a swim. I wanted to check with you that it was all right to take him,' Emily said.

Romeo eyed Maisie with one brow quirked.

She lifted her chin. 'I'll take him,' she answered. When his eyes narrowed, she sighed. 'We'll *both* take him?' she amended.

The corner of his mouth twitched. *'Grazie,'* he murmured.

Maisie nodded. 'Okay. I'll go and change.'

Romeo strode forward and caught Lucca up in his arms. 'We'll meet you by the pool.'

In her room, Maisie fingered her sensible one-piece suit, replaying the conversation with Romeo in her mind. He'd been surprised that she'd returned to look for him, more than surprised, in fact. Stunned. That she would want to do the right thing.

Again she found herself wondering just how damaging his relationship with his mother had been. He'd called her a whore in the car. Had he meant that *literally*? She shuddered. Why else would a child call his mother by such a derogatory term?

It was clear that Romeo Brunetti had huge skeletons in his closet. And she was treading on dangerous ground in being so interested in uncovering them. That he'd taken such drastic steps to disconnect himself from her after their single night together should warn her that he didn't want any entanglements that didn't involve his son. She would do well to remember that. Along with remembering that theirs would in no way be a physical merger. No matter how heatedly he looked at her. No matter how much her blood thrilled to insane sexual possibilities each time he was within touching distance.

There would come a time when she'd have to walk away with her son after all this was done.

She would be better off if she made sure to walk away with her heart intact.

Romeo noticed her cooler demeanour the moment she came down the terrace steps and walked through the leafy archway dividing the extensive barbecue and entertainment area from the pool. And it had nothing to do with the military-issue swimming suit she wore, or the tight knot she'd pulled her hair into at the top of her head.

Her gaze, when it skated over him, was wary. As if between the time they'd spoken in his study and her changing, she'd withdrawn into herself.

Had she somehow guessed at his true intention towards his son when this problem with Lorenzo was over?

No, there was no way she could know. He quashed the voice in his head that prompted him to recall Maisie's uncanny intuitiveness. She'd known just how to delve beneath his skin and burrow to the heart of his need that night five years ago.

She'd given him passion and compassion in abundance, two emotions that had been seriously lacking in his life up till then. She'd made him *believe* and *hope*, for a few blissful hours, until dawn and reality had come crashing in. For a while he'd resented her for those feelings. Until he'd realised the fault wasn't hers. It was him, daring to believe in mirages and miracles.

He watched her drop her sunglasses on the table and walk to the edge of the pool, her smile guarded as she observed Lucca's antics. For the first time in his life, Romeo experienced the need to enquire as to a woman's feelings. The unsettled feelings that had slashed through him in the car returned and grew as he watched her swim to the other end of the pool and stay there.

Normally, when the women he dated began exhibiting contrary attitudes, it was a prelude to them asking for *more*. Of his time. Of a commitment. It was the reason he'd drastically reduced his dating span from a few weeks to the odd weekend.

He had nothing more to offer a woman besides a good time in bed and a very generous parting gift come Monday morning.

So what did Maisie's attitude mean?

She had his ring on her finger. Albeit temporarily, and for the sake of their son. But she also had him here, far from civilisation should they choose, and as exclusive as resorts came. And if and when she chose to alter the terms of their non-physical relationship to a physical one, he was more than willing to negotiate.

So what was wrong?

'Faster, faster!' Lucca urged as he rode on Romeo's back. 'Mummy, let's race.' He held out his arms to his mother. Maisie smiled and swam towards them, but she still avoided Romeo's gaze. And kept a conspicuous distance between them as they splashed from one end of the pool to the other.

Eventually, he took a tired and protesting Lucca out of the water. Maisie followed them out and dried him, before taking him indoors. When she returned and perched on her lounger with that same air of withdrawal, he narrowed his eyes.

'I don't like mixed signals,' he snapped.

Her head jerked towards him. 'What?'

'You were fine when you left the study. Something has obviously happened between then and now. What is it?'

'Nothing. I just took a little time to think, that's all.'

Something tightened in his chest, but he forced out the question. 'And what did thinking produce?'

She flashed a bright, false smile. 'I concluded that you're

right. Lucca and I have never had a holiday. This will be good for him...for all of us. As long as I can find something to keep me busy at times, I won't stand in your way about the small things.'

He heard the words and processed them as the half-truth they were. Then sat back and formulated how to get the full truth out of her.

CHAPTER EIGHT

'WE'RE HEADING OUT to choose a venue for a duck pond. You said you'd join us.' Romeo used a tone that made it clear his request wasn't up for debate. His annoyance the past few days had grown into a simmering anger. Albeit that anger was directed more at himself for the unaccustomed feeling of *caring* so much.

But some of it was directed at the woman who raised her head from her video conversation with her friend in Dublin and looked at him with a blank stare.

He'd been on the receiving end of that stare every time he walked into a room, just as every time he came within touching distance she found a way to move away. He'd thought she would be happy when he'd arranged for her to work with the chef at the resort restaurant a few hours each day to keep her skills sharp. She'd been pleased and his chef had sung her praises, but Maisie continued to be aloof.

Enough was enough. He wanted that distance gone.

The voice that suggested he might live to regret closing that distance was ruthlessly suppressed. He strolled further into the room and stopped in front of her, arms folded. 'Our son is waiting.'

Satisfaction burst through him when her eyes lit up with rebellious fire.

'Um…sorry, Bronagh, I have to go. I'll be in touch again at the end of the week.' She smiled and signed off, then glared up at him. 'Was there any need to be so rude?'

'Perhaps you should ask yourself the same question.'

A frown marred the light, golden hue of her skin, the result of enjoying the Hawaiian sun. 'What on earth are you talking about?'

'You've called your friend three times since we got here. You don't think she'd be offended that you're micromanaging her from a distance?'

Her eyes widened. 'Of course not, we discussed me calling her before I left Dublin.'

'Every other day?'

'Maybe not, but—'

'What percentage of your call involved discussing the restaurant?'

She bit her lip and flushed bright red. 'That still doesn't excuse your rudely interrupting me.'

'I'm only doing what you asked, *gattina*, and reminding you that you said you'd come with us to view the site. If you've changed your mind, all you have to do is say so. Lucca would be disappointed, of course, but...' Romeo shrugged.

She frowned and checked the clock on the laptop. 'I haven't changed my mind. I just didn't realise what the time was, that's all.' She looked at him and her gaze swung away almost immediately. 'I...I'll be right there.'

He narrowed his eyes when she remained seated. 'Is there a problem I should know about?' he grated, realising he was reaching the end of a hitherto unknown rope of patience.

'No.' Her lower lip protruded in an annoyed action so reminiscent of their son that he almost laughed. But his annoyance was far greater than his mirth. And it grew the longer she remained seated.

'Do I need to eject you from that chair?' he asked softly.

Her loose, waist-length hair slid over her shoulders as she swivelled her chair sideways. 'I only meant that I'd meet you outside after I get changed.'

He assessed her blue vest top. 'There's nothing wrong with what you're wearing.'

Her colour rose higher. 'Not the top maybe, but the shorts aren't appropriate for going outside.'

Romeo's legs moved of their own accord, skirting the desk to where she sat. 'Stand up.'

She threw him another of those highly annoyed looks but reluctantly stood.

He nearly swallowed his tongue.

The bright pink hot pants moulded her hips like a second skin and ended a scant inch below where the material met between her thighs. Instant arousal like nothing he'd ever experienced before battered him so hard, he was sure his insides had been rearranged in the process.

'Che diavolo,' he managed to squeeze out when he dragged his gaze from that triangle of temptation between her thighs and the silky smooth length of her shapely legs to her bare feet and up again.

'Don't blame me,' she muttered with husky accusation. 'It's not my fault your personal shoppers got my size wrong. If you'd let me go with them like I suggested, none of this would've happened.'

He met her impossibly blue eyes with a stunned exhalation. 'Are you telling me *all* your clothes are too small?'

He'd had a new wardrobe organised for Maisie and Lucca when it had become apparent that she'd packed clothes suitable for an Irish summer, not the tropical Hawaiian heat. And he for one had been tired of Maisie's ugly swimsuit after seeing it a second time.

She lifted her hand to fiddle with her hair and a glimpse of her toned midriff sent his temperature soaring another thousand degrees. 'They're a size smaller than I'd normally prefer.'

'And you didn't say something because?' He was aware his voice was uneven, hell, *strangled*, and that continuing to stand this close to her while she was dressed like a naughty cheerleader was an immensely bad idea, but his feet refused to move anywhere but closer, the need to slide his fingers between her legs, test the heat of those hot pants, almost overpowering.

'Would I have sounded anything but a diva if I'd demanded they send everything back?'

Since he knew every single one of the women he'd dated before would've made exactly that demand, and more, he allowed himself a smile. 'You're my wife. You're well within your rights to demand anything you want, as often as you want.'

She seemed to grow unsteady, her hand reaching out blindly for the sturdiness of the desk. But her gaze didn't move from his, an action for which he felt almost elated. Romeo couldn't take in how much he'd missed looking into her eyes until that moment. Which was absurd, but unshakeably true.

'It's okay, it's not a big deal. I can get away with most of the tops and dresses, and I'd planned to only wear the shorts indoors.' She licked her lips and laughed a touch nervously. 'Besides, I can stand to lose a pound or ten.'

'*Nothing* about your body requires adjustment,' he growled.

She was perfect. And she was blushing in the full-bodied way again that was pure combustion to his libido.

His eyes dropped to where she was winding one leg around the other, her toes brushing her opposite insole. Hunger clawed through him.

Madre di Dio!

'Go. Change if you must. We'll be waiting out front,' he forced out before the unbearable need pounding through him overcame his better judgement and he bent her over the desk.

She nodded and backed away, turning to hurry out of the door. When he was sure she was out of earshot, he let out a thick, frustrated groan, the sight of her delicious backside seeming to tattoo itself in his mind.

He was nowhere near calm when she emerged in a strapless lilac sundress and flip-flops. Luckily for him, his son's presence served as enough of a deterrent for his out-of-control libido.

Ten minutes later, it became clear she'd gone back to not fully engaging with him, busying herself with fussing over Lucca and avoiding his eyes when he looked her way.

Gritting his teeth, he focused on delivering them to the first duck-pond scouting location.

They toured three sites before arriving at the perfect place for a duck pond. Well within sight of the villa, the area was flat and clear of trees, within full view of the beach. Not that Lucca would ever be alone, but Romeo was satisfied the security posted at various points around the island would have a perfect view of where Maisie and his son were at all times.

The head of the three-man construction crew he'd hired spread out the blueprint on a portable table and began discussing design and schedules, with Lucca merrily pointing out where he wanted his rocks and fountain situated.

Leaving them to it, Romeo strolled to where Maisie stood several feet away, her gaze on the beach a quarter of a mile below.

Her head jerked up as he neared, and she inhaled sharply at the force of his stare, her eyes widening before she attempted to avert her head. He caught her chin and held her still.

'You want to tell me what's going on?'

That blank stare again. 'Sorry, I don't know what you mean.'

'I thought we agreed to make this work,' he rasped.

'We are.'

'You call *this* making it work?' he blazed under his breath.

'Romeo, why are you annoyed with me?'

His low mocking laughter grated. 'I suppose I should be gratified that you've noticed that I am annoyed.'

She pulled her chin from his hand. 'If it's about me forgetting about the time of the duck-pond visit—'

'Don't do that, *gattina*. It's beneath you,' he cut across her.

'I don't know what you want me to do. I'm here for Lucca. Isn't that what we both ultimately want?' Her voice pulsed with something he couldn't put his finger on.

No, he wanted to say. *I want you to stop shutting me out.*

He stepped closer and her delicate apple shampoo and sunflower perfume washed over his senses. 'What he needs is parents who exchange more than a greeting and a "pass the salt" when they're in the same room. I may not know enough about little boys yet, but I know he'll pick up the tension between us if we don't clear the air.'

She shook her head. 'But there *is* nothing to clear.'

He begged to differ. About to demand the truth, he looked deeper into her eyes and finally got *why* the atmosphere between them had altered so drastically.

'*Dio*, how could I have missed this?' he muttered almost to himself.

Panic flared in her eyes, darkening the striking blue to an alluring navy. He allowed himself a smile, a little less unsettled now he knew the root cause of her frostiness.

'We'll take this up again tonight, when Lucca is in bed.'

'I have nothing to take up with you,' she blurted.

'Then you can enjoy your meal and listen to me talk.'

Enjoying the heated suspicion in her eyes, he turned and strode back to join the group. The final design of the pond was agreed, an ecstatic Lucca skipping back to the buggy.

Back at the villa, he watched Maisie rush away with an excuse of rustling up a snack for their son. Romeo curbed a smile, satisfied now that he knew what the problem was of fixing it. He was pussyfooting his way through the unfamiliar landscape of being a father. The tension between him and Maisie stood to jeopardise that. The unnecessary argument in his study this afternoon had proved that. It

needed to be resolved. And by midnight, the situation between them *would* be rectified, with results he was sure
would please them both.

He picked up his son and hurled him in the air, his heart
tumbling over when he received a shriek of delight in return.

'Again!' Lucca urged.

Romeo's smile widened and he complied.

He'd never relied on luck to achieve his goals, but with
a tiny bit of luck he'd get his son's mother shrieking those
same words to him by the time he was done with her.

Maisie inspected the multitude of new dresses in her wardrobe and finally selected a bronze-coloured cotton shift with
a crossover bodice tie. She knew she was risking being late,
but ever since her conversation with Romeo earlier she'd
been dreading the seven-thirty dinner he'd asked Mahina
to prepare.

To say she was terrified of that sudden light that had
dawned in his eyes after he'd demanded to know what was
going on would be an understatement. And that self-assured
smile he'd worn from then on had been an even more ominous sign that whatever he intended to discuss with her tonight would be something she might not be able to deny him.

She tied the knot beneath the bodice of the dress and
shakily clipped her hair into a loose knot at her nape. The
sleeveless design of the dress would ensure she remained
cool in the sometimes sultry evening heat.

And if all hell broke loose, there was also the swimming
pool to jump into. She gave a short hysterical giggle and
slipped her feet into open-toed platform heels.

Knowing she couldn't linger any longer, she hurried to
Lucca's room and checked on him, smiling at Emily, who
was folding laundry in the walk-in closet, before making
her way to the terrace.

The light from fat candles giving off evocative scents
blended with solar lamps dotted around the garden and pool.

Next to the table set out for two, a tall silver ice bucket held a bottle of champagne. Romeo was nowhere in sight.

Before she could breathe a sigh of relief from the nerves churning her stomach, she sensed him behind her and turned.

He was dressed in black trousers and a fitted black shirt, his sleeves rolled back to reveal bronzed forearms and a sleek watch. With a few buttons opened at his throat, it was impossible to miss the light wisps of hair or the strong neck and the rugged jaw thrown into relief by all that black. That image of a dark lord, master of all he surveyed, sprang into her mind again.

Maisie swallowed and willed her hormones to stop careening through her bloodstream. But even at this early stage in the night, she knew it would be an uphill battle to continue fighting the need that whistled through her with the ominous sound of a pressure cooker reaching explosion point.

'There you are,' he murmured in a deep, hypnotic voice. 'I was beginning to think I'd been stood up.'

'I wasn't aware this was a date,' she replied feebly. The setting sun, the soft Hawaiian music playing from hidden speakers…the way he looked at her, all pointed to this being all about the two of them and nothing to do with their son.

She took a tiny step back as he came towards her, all dark and brooding. His eyes told her he knew what she was fighting. And the calculating gleam told her he intended to make sure she would lose.

'Come, sit down.'

He walked past her, trailing an earthy scent of spicy sandalwood and his own potent musk that drew her like a supercharged bee to pollen, and pulled out a chair.

With a feeling of walking towards her doom, Maisie approached and took her seat, then gasped when his fingers trailed the back of her neck.

'You must be more careful in the sun, *gattina*. You have mild sunburn right here.'

She shivered and touched the slightly sore spot, berating herself for being disappointed because his touch had been for an impersonal reason. 'September in Palermo was the hottest weather I'd encountered before Hawaii. I think I might need a stronger sunscreen.'

He sat opposite her, his gaze thoughtful as it rested on her face.

As Mahina served their first course, she held her breath, knowing questions were coming from Romeo.

As soon as the housekeeper left, he asked, 'You never took holidays abroad when you were younger?'

She shook her head. 'There was never time for holidays. Or any free time for that matter. Dedication to my studies seven days a week from kindergarten till I graduated from law school saw to that.'

His eyes narrowed. 'Your parents demanded this of you?'

'Yes.'

When she didn't elaborate further, he pressed. 'Tell me about them.'

'I thought our pasts were out of bounds?'

Reaching for the chilling bottle, he poured her a drink before serving himself. 'They are, but I seem to have shared a lot of mine with you without meaning to. I think it's time we address the imbalance.'

Looking away from him for a moment, she contemplated the last of the lingering orange-and-purple sunset and the stars already beginning to make an appearance.

She didn't want to talk about her parents, or the single-minded ambition that drove them and had made her childhood an endless drudge of trying, and failing, to please them.

And yet, she found herself nodding.

CHAPTER NINE

SHE PICKED UP her fork and tasted the exotic fruit and prawn salad, and busied herself with chewing while pushing her food around on her plate as she struggled to find the right words.

'My parents knew very early on that I wasn't academically gifted as they were—they're both Fulbright scholars and prize academic excellence above everything else.'

'Including you?' he asked astutely.

She swallowed and answered without looking up. 'Including me. I was an accident, who turned even more burdensome when I was unable to fulfil my full potential in their eyes.' When he didn't respond, she risked a glance.

His face was set in a carefully blank expression, but she glimpsed a look in his eyes, a *kinship*, that made her throat clog.

Clearing it, she continued. 'To say they were stunned their genius hadn't been replicated in me was an understatement. I was five when they made me take my first IQ test. They refused to believe the result. I took one every year until I was fifteen, when they finally accepted that I wouldn't be anything more than slightly above average.'

She sipped her champagne, let it wash away the bitter knowledge that she would always be a disappointment in her parents' eyes.

'Did they stop pushing you at this point?' he enquired sharply after helping himself to the last morsel on his plate.

Her mouth twisted. 'On the contrary. They pushed me harder with the belief that as long as they continued to polish me I would turn into the diamond they wanted instead of the unacceptable cubic zirconia.'

'I disagree with that description of yourself, and the assessment that you're average, but go on,' he encouraged, lounging back, all drop-dead-gorgeous danger, to nurse his drink as their first course was cleared away.

She shrugged. 'There's nothing much to add to that. They were indifferent to everything in my life besides my academic achievements, such as they were. When I told them I wanted to be a lawyer, they grudgingly accepted my decision, then immediately started pulling strings for me to be hired by one of the Magic Circle law firms in the country. When I told them I was taking three months off and then returning to take a position at a firm in Dublin, our relationship strained even more.'

'But you didn't back down?'

She laughed bitterly. 'It's hard being an average child of two geniuses, who hadn't wanted a child in the first place. I guess I'd reached a point where I'd had enough.' She'd wanted to lash out, rebel against the oppressive weight of her parents' indifference. Palermo had been her moment of rebellion. And while she would never regret having Lucca, she was beginning to be afraid that the one man she'd rebelled with had set a benchmark for all other men to come. And that each and every one of them would be found wanting.

She drank some more, felt the bubbles buzz through her veins and loosen her tongue. She even managed a less strained smile when Mahina delivered their second course.

'I presume that three-month vacation included your stop in Palermo?' he asked when they were alone again.

With the unburdening of her past came an unexpected increase in appetite. Or it could've been the alcohol.

Shrugging inwardly, Maisie tucked into the grilled mahi mahi and gave an appreciative moan. 'Yes. I'd always been fascinated with all things Italian.' She paused, glanced at him and saw the mildly mocking brow he lifted in her direction. Flushing, she returned her attention to her plate. 'I had some money saved from when I worked part-time at uni, and toured the whole of Italy. Palermo was my third stop.'

'And did your relationship improve once you resumed your career?' he asked. His questions weren't prying, as she supposed hers had been. He seemed to be interested in her life, her past, and not just as a means of passing time at the dinner table.

So she found herself recounting the one painful event in her life she'd sworn never to revisit again. 'Not once they found out I was pregnant by a man whose last name I didn't even know. Both my mother and father came from broken homes. They were estranged from their parents by the time I grew up. I know they hadn't planned on getting married, but they did because my mother fell pregnant with me. When I in turn got pregnant, the confirmation that the apple truly didn't fall far from the tree was too much for them to stomach.' The words fell from her lips in sharp bursts, the pain she'd smothered away in her heart rising to stab her once again.

She chanced a glance at Romeo and saw that he had frozen, his face a taut, forbidding mask.

'So they severed ties with you?' he asked in a chilling voice.

'Not exactly. But they had views on how to bring up Lucca that I didn't welcome.'

'What views?'

'They wanted me to put him in the care of nannies to start, and then boarding school when he was four—'

Romeo's curse stemmed the flow of her narrative. 'So he wouldn't get in the way of your career?' he bit out.

'Yes,' she replied, her throat painful with the admission that no matter what she achieved, she wouldn't be worthy in her parents' eyes.

His breath hissed out in pure rage. *'Madonna mia,'* he sliced out, his nostrils flaring as he struggled to control himself. 'Did you consider it?' he asked with a narrow-eyed stare.

'No. I gave up my job, enrolled in a gourmet cooking course, then moved to Ranelagh to open the restaurant.'

A morose silence fell over the table, their half-eaten meal growing cold as the sharp cries of cicadas pierced the night.

'This wasn't how I planned this evening unfolding,' Romeo said several minutes later after he'd refilled her glass.

Maisie laughed self-deprecatingly, that buzz in her veins somehow making the pain throbbing in her chest sharper. She was sure it was light-headedness that made her enquire breezily, 'So how had you planned this evening going, then?'

He didn't answer for a long time. Then he stood, tall, imposing, breathtaking. 'Come, we'll walk on the beach for a while.' He grabbed his glass and the half-finished bottle in one hand and held out his other. 'Let the night air wash away unpalatable memories.'

Maisie knew she ought to refuse, that the alcohol swirling through her bloodstream would inhibit any rational decisions she needed to make.

And yet she found herself sliding her hand into his, rising to her feet and discarding her shoes when he instructed her to.

The walk to the beach was lazy, the sultry night air and soft ukulele-threaded music emerging from hidden speakers seeming to slow everything down to a heavy, sensual, irresistible tempo.

He let go of her hand when they reached the sand, filled their glasses with the last of the champagne, then walked a few feet away to dispose of the bottle.

Toes curling in the warm sand, she strolled to the water's edge, laughing softly when the cool water splashed over her feet.

For a single moment, Maisie dared to wonder how it

would be to be in this place with the man of her dreams under different circumstances; if she'd been on a real honeymoon, not a desperate attempt to thwart a wizened old thug's threats.

The path her parents had set her on as a child hadn't left much room for dreaming. She'd been too busy trying to earn their love, to make herself worthy of their acceptance, to entertain such flights of fancy.

But she was a grown woman now, and surely there was nothing wrong with letting her imagination run wild for a few minutes, in letting her senses be overwhelmed by this beautiful place, this breathtaking man beside her?

She drained her second glass and didn't protest when Romeo took it away, then returned to stand behind her. Her breath shuddered out when he slid his hands over her shoulders and started a gentle massage of the tension-knotted muscles.

'What are you doing, Romeo?' she asked shakily after several minutes, when she started to melt beneath the warm kneading.

'You're tense. Why?'

'Probably because you're touching me.'

'You were tense before I touched you. Did I do something to make you this way?'

She released a single bark of laughter. 'The whole world doesn't revolve around you, Romeo.'

'Perhaps not, but if there's a problem going on with you it needs to be addressed, do you not agree?' He turned her around, looked into her face and frowned. 'Are you bored? Do you require more challenges?'

'No, I'm finding the lessons with Chef Sylvain illuminating and Mahina is teaching me a few Tongan recipes that will come in handy when I return to Ranelagh.'

His mouth compressed but he nodded. 'But you're not happy. Don't deny it.'

She tried to step out of his hypnotising sphere, but he held her by the elbows.

'This afternoon you thought you knew what ailed me.'

His gaze sharpened, then he gave a wry smile. 'Maybe it was my own need talking.'

'What…what need?'

'The need that claws beneath my skin, threatens to eat me alive…'

She made a barely audible sound when he pulled the clip from her hair and the heavy knot tumbled over her shoulders. Strong fingers slid through her hair in slow, sensual caresses. Maisie realised her dream was sliding dangerously into a yearning for reality that would be hard to push back in a bottle should she set it free.

But still she stayed, moaning softly when his mouth brushed the sensitive and tender spot below her ear. Light kisses traced along her jaw, down her neck to the pulse hammering at her throat. Desire pounded her, making her limbs heavy and the need to maintain that distance she'd been struggling to achieve melt away.

He spun her into his arms, and she gasped at the voracious hunger stamped on his face.

'Romeo…'

His kiss stopped whatever feeble attempt she'd been scrambling for to save herself from the unstoppable freight train of sexual fury that hurtled towards her. But as he took control of her mouth, control of her body, Maisie knew she would welcome being taken over, being flattened by the sheer force of his hunger, as long as it satisfied hers.

And it would.

From searing memory, she knew Romeo was an unselfish lover. If anything, he achieved a deeper level of arousal by piling on her pleasure, taking her to the very brink of sexual release and burning with her as they both fell.

He would give her everything her body desperately craved. And more.

But what happened next? What of tomorrow?

The questions began like small, icy kernels at the back of her mind. Then loomed, snowballed, until she pushed at his chest, desperate to free herself of this illusion.

'Stop!'

He raised his head immediately but didn't release her. 'You want me. Don't bother denying it,' he lashed out at her, his body vibrating with the tension that would surely explode at any moment.

His gaze dropped to her lips when she licked them, savouring the taste of him to pathetically add to her collection of memories.

'Yes, I do. But I won't let you use me to scratch an itch that only stems out of being thrown together more than anything else.'

He cursed under his breath. 'What's that supposed to mean?'

'It means we have a thing for each other, I won't deny that. But it's meaningless. Just a brand of chemistry that will probably go away if we ignore it. I'm not going to experiment on something cheap and tawdry just because we both happen to have time on our hands. I have more self-worth than that.'

He dropped his hands and took a single step back, but his dark gold eyes stayed on her. Accusing. Condemning. 'We took marriage vows. I think that elevates anything that happens between us well above cheap and tawdry.'

'Please don't do that. Don't rewrite the script on what the end goal is here. We only got married because of Lucca. And we agreed there would be no physical manifestation of those vows. Don't change the terms now.'

He laughed mockingly. 'You talk to me about changing the terms when you can't be in the same room as me or have a simple conversation without your pulse jumping all over the place?'

Heat suffused her face, along with anger. 'So you thought

you'd take pity on your sexually frustrated wife and do something about it?' she threw at him. 'How very stoic of you.'

'If I recall, leaving the physical side out of the marriage was your decision. I merely agreed because you seemed strongly wedded to the idea, pun intended. There's no shame in requesting a renegotiation.'

'I'm not requesting anything! All this...' she waved her hand at the sandy beach, the jaw-droppingly gorgeous moonlight and the discarded champagne bottle and glasses '...was your doing. Some sort of attempt at seduction, perhaps?'

He fisted his hair and then released it with a Latin flourish that made her belly quiver against her will.

'Only because I thought it wise to tackle the situation before one of us exploded,' he growled, his cheekbones hollowing out as he glared at her.

'Well, consider it tackled. I'll endeavour to keep my *desires* under better control from now on.'

The tension in his body was so palpable, she could almost reach out and touch it.

'You do realise there are millions of married couples who actually have sex with each other? Why not us?'

A shiver went through her, but she still managed to lift her chin and face that challenge head-on. 'Because I'm not built to have emotionless sex,' she flamed at him, at the end of her tether. 'And I'm damn sure you know that, Romeo. So stop. Please...just stop!'

Burnished gold eyes gleamed with such intensity, Maisie feared she might have poked the lion one too many times. For several seconds he just stared at her, hands on hips, his gaze probing to her very soul.

A heavy sigh depressed his chest, then he nodded solemnly. 'I will stop if you want me to. But I think we both know it won't be that easy, *gattina*. Come and find me when you change your mind.'

CHAPTER TEN

SHE MADE IT through the next seven days. Even went as far as to pat herself on the back for her stellar performance. Even when her body threatened resistance and advocated surrender at every turn, Maisie ground her teeth and sallied forth.

She looked into Romeo's eyes when he addressed her; didn't move away when he approached to discuss whatever was on his mind, or dance away as she normally would've when they took turns teaching Lucca to swim.

Even when she began to suspect that Romeo was deliberately testing her resolve by standing too close when they watched a particularly stunning sunset, or when his fingers lingered a touch too long when he passed her a plate of fruit at the breakfast table.

In those times she forced herself to remember how transient this situation was. And that the end might come sooner rather than later. He'd opened up when she'd heard him having a heated phone call two nights after their escapade on the beach.

Lorenzo had finally come out and demanded a cash settlement to restore the *famiglia's* dwindling power. Romeo had flatly refused.

The old man had retreated.

Whether that was merely a distraction tactic was something Romeo was investigating, but so far they had nothing concrete to indict him with. But if it proved not to be, then Lucca could be well out of danger before his fourth birthday next week. They hadn't discussed what would happen afterwards and she'd presumed Romeo would want access to his son, but Maisie couldn't see the man who'd been labelled the Weekend Lover, the same man who'd walked away from her so definitely five years ago, wanting to remain tied down through a marriage licence.

Her heart lurched painfully and she turned from watching Romeo and Lucca splashing on the other side of the pool. She thought of her little flat in Ranelagh and immediately hated herself for thinking it would be dull and dreary compared to this brilliant paradise. Compared to living under the same roof as Romeo.

Ranelagh was her home. One she was proud of.

She'd survived putting Romeo behind her five years ago. As painful as it'd been, she'd survived walking away from parents who would never love her the way she knew parents should love their child.

She would get through this when the time came.

'Is this your new way of attempting to tune me out? Staring out to sea and hoping you'll be turned into a mermaid?' His low voice seared along her nerve endings, starting that infernal flame that would only build the longer he stayed close.

She looked around and saw Emily walking off with a tired Lucca. Once they'd settled into a routine, Maisie had come round to the idea of letting Emily help with Lucca. They got on well, and Maisie could indulge in honing her culinary skills without guilt.

Bracing herself, she met Romeo's dark hazel eyes, the blazing sexual fire he no longer attempted to hide evident in his return stare.

'How very arrogant of you to assume my every thought revolves around you,' she replied coolly, although cool was the last thing she felt when he was this close, his arms braced on either side of the pool wall, caging her in.

'When I'm with you, like this, I guarantee that every one of mine revolves around you,' he supplied in a whispered breath.

Maisie suppressed a shiver. 'If you're trying to get me to crawl into your bed like a pathetic little sex slave, forget it.'

'There's nothing remotely pathetic about you, *gattina*. When you *do* crawl into my bed, I imagine you'll be a fierce little warrior woman.' He moved closer, his warm, chiselled torso sliding against her back in the water. 'Don't make me wait too long, though.'

Her fingers clung to the edge of the pool, her knuckles turning white with the effort. 'Or what?' she whispered fiercely. Daringly.

'Or your wildcat ways will be met with a much more predatory force than would be wise for either of us,' he breathed.

'Romeo, don't.'

It was then she felt the barely leashed dominance of his whole body. His powerful erection nudged her bottom, its hard and thick promise making her shut her eyes and bite back the helpless, hungry moan that rose to her lips.

'You think sex between us will be emotionless?' he queried in a harsh whisper.

She shook her head. 'What else can it be?'

'It wasn't five years ago. You had enough passion for both of us, and more. And I gave you what you needed. This time, we're husband and wife. You can let it count for something or you can let the transient nature of our situation stop you from demanding what you want. What we both want. Think about that, Maisie.'

The next second, he was swimming away, hauling himself out of the water like an arrogant god. He didn't look her way again as he towelled off and entered the villa.

Maisie stayed put, fighting the need to surrender with every last atom in her body, fiercely resisting the knowledge that the uphill battle with herself where Romeo was concerned was only just starting. And that this time, she risked losing more than just her dignity.

* * *

As Romeo had instructed all week, they dined outside, between sunset and when the stars came out. She kept the conversation on safe topics, determined to stay away from the bombshell he'd placed between them at the pool.

We're husband and wife.

The yearning those words triggered in her was something she didn't want to dwell on.

'The builders assure me the work will be done by the weekend. Which is just as well because I think our son has reached the point where we'll wake up one morning and find him down there finishing the pond with his own two hands.' The words were delivered with a bracing amount of amused dread.

Maisie laughed. 'I think poor Emily's at her wits' end, too, with reassuring him the pond will be ready by his birthday. If he decides to finish it on his own, I think she might help him, just for the sake of achieving some peace.'

Romeo smiled, and his face was transformed from brooding sexiness to heart-stopping so fast her heart took a dizzy dive. 'I suppose it's a blessing then he's managed to twist her around his fingers so soon. I can foresee a time when she adores him as much as we do.'

He froze suddenly and his breath caught. The eyes that met hers held stunned shock and when he reached for his red wine, she saw how his hand trembled.

She laid her hand over his as a lump rose in her throat. 'It's okay to admit you love your son, Romeo,' she said gently. 'In fact, I think it's time you told him as much, and that you're his father.'

The shock dissipated, replaced by the customary brooding. He eyed her with a mildly disparaging look. 'So was this some sort of test?'

She jerked her hand away. 'Excuse me?'

'To see how I fared in the fatherhood stakes before offering your permission to let him know I'm his father?' he tagged on.

'Of course not,' she replied, the barb stinging deep and painfully. 'You really think so little of me? Or of yourself?' she added, because she sensed some of that pointed remark was directed at himself.

A fleeting expression flashed across his face, almost like regret. Then his features tightened. 'Why would you think any more of me or my fathering skills? You know enough about my background to know I have no experience in this. That my own childhood has left scars I'll never be able to erase. Scars that could manifest in unpredictable ways somewhere down the line.'

She frowned. 'What do you mean?'

His mouth pursed for so long she thought he wouldn't answer. 'You know I lived on the streets. What you don't know is that I joined a gang a few years after that. One that even the authorities feared to tackle.'

Unease climbed into her throat. 'Why?'

'Because I wanted to fit in, *somewhere*.'

The raw vulnerability caught at her heart. 'And did you?'

He exhaled harshly. 'Not after I refused to perform the initiation rites.'

'Which were?'

Her heart froze as he enunciated what he'd been asked to do. Silence settled over their table, until he raised his head.

'You see why fatherhood isn't a job I'm to be trusted to settle into easily.'

Maisie's heart squeezed at the pain in his voice. 'But you walked away. You chose to walk away instead of hurting another human being.'

'That doesn't mean I'm equipped to handle this!'

'You're fighting Lorenzo instead of giving in to threats and extortion. You swore to protect Lucca within hours of meeting him. You've done nothing but care for him since we got here. Doesn't that tell you something? Love makes you vulnerable sometimes, but it doesn't make you weak.'

His mouth twisted, but the pain in his eyes dissipated a little. 'I wouldn't know. Lucca's young now, adorable and easy to handle. Who's to say what will come later, and how well we'll handle it?' His voice was thin and a touch bleak, holding echoes of his past.

Her hands clenched on the pristine white tablecloth. 'Stop borrowing trouble, Romeo. You've done well so far. Let's just take it one day at a time. And if you're not ready to tell Lucca that you're his father, then we'll wait.'

A muscle flexed in this jaw. 'I wanted to tell him who I was the first moment I knew he was mine.'

The touch of frost inside her melted. 'Fine. Tomorrow, then, or the day after. Whenever you're ready.'

His mouth compressed for several seconds. Then he nodded. *'Bene.'*

Maisie swallowed and nodded in return. She started to reach for her water glass, but he caught her hand in his.

'I'm sorry for not handling this better.'

The remaining frost was replaced by dizzying warmth. 'It's okay. I muddle through motherhood every day.' She smiled.

He raised her hand to his lips and kissed the soft skin. 'You've done an admirable job, *gattina.'*

Heat unfurled in her stomach, wending its way through her body when he continued to caress her with his mouth.

She cleared her throat and forced herself to say something before she crumbled beneath the smouldering onslaught. 'And you've had more experience than I think you're letting on.'

His eyebrows rose.

'There was a picture of you in the paper, on a yacht with two little boys,' she pried gently.

A look crossed his face, a facsimile of the one he wore whenever he interacted with his son. 'Rafa and Carlo are

Zaccheo's twin sons, and my godsons.' He shrugged. 'At least that's what it says on paper. I don't really have much interaction with them.'

'Zaccheo is your ex-business partner?'

He hesitated for a moment, then nodded. '*Sì*, but he is more than that.'

'In what way?'

Hazel eyes darkened a touch. 'Our pasts were inter-twined for a brief time during which we formed an unlikely bond.' His tone suggested he wouldn't elaborate, but as she had before, Maisie couldn't help but pry, her need to know this man inside and out a yearning that wouldn't go away.

'Before or after you lived on the streets?'

'Before. Zaccheo's parents took me in for a while, but that situation could never be anything but temporary because my presence in their lives was not their choice.'

He turned her hand over, his fingers tracing her palm in slow, lazy circles. It wasn't a sensual move, even though there was plenty of that arcing between them. It was a grounding touch that sought, and received, a connection.

'Are you ever going to tell me what happened with your mother?' she murmured.

He froze immediately. 'I don't consider the subject suit-able dinner conversation.'

She sighed. 'Then I guess, since dinner is over, I should retire to bed.'

'So you can tuck yourself into your cool sheets and con-gratulate yourself for escaping this needless torture you in-sist on putting us both through?' he grated at her, a different, more dangerous brooding taking over his face. She also de-tected a vulnerability that made her wonder whether there was something more going on here than she was aware of.

She slowly pulled her hand away. 'It's not needless.'

His mouth twisted. 'I suppose it's something that you don't deny it's torturous.' He caught up his glass and drained the last of his wine. The precision with which he set down the exquisite crystal made her think he would very much like to launch it across the terrace floor and watch it shatter in a million pieces.

He shoved his chair back and stood. 'Perhaps I'll take a leaf out of your book and live in denial for a while. I'm sure there's an urgent business decision I need to make somewhere in my company. Sleep well, *gattina*,' he said mockingly, before striding off in the direction of his study.

She knew the mocking command would have the opposite effect even before she undressed and slid into bed two hours later after giving up the pretence of reading.

Tossing and turning, Maisie tried rationalising and re-affirming her decisions. When by the thousandth time her own reasoning sounded mockingly hollow, she gave up. Frustrated, she yanked back the sheets and sat up. The hot-pink silk negligee she wore felt sticky on her skin, but the warm night air was inviting, a great way to empty her thoughts of the disturbing feeling that her resistance was crumbling.

Tugging the silk over her head, she went into her dressing room and rummaged through the drawer containing her new selection of swimwear. When her fingers closed over an as-yet-unworn set, she pulled out the string bikini she'd looked at and immediately discarded when her wardrobe had arrived. Of all the swimwear that had been delivered, this was the most daring. The cups of the top part of the black-and-orange set barely covered half her breasts and the matching panties were made of nothing more than three pieces of string, leaving very little to the imagination.

Making a face, she set it aside. Then glanced back at it. The little thrill of naughtiness surged higher the longer she eyed the garment.

She was tired of being sensible. Especially at one o'clock in the morning. Deciding to add a little bit of spice to her illicit swim, she quickly donned the bikini and threw a white linen tunic over it.

The villa was quiet, and she breathed a sigh of relief as she passed Romeo's empty study.

The path to the waterfall was softly lit by garden lamps. Snagging a towel from the stack near the swimming pool, she skirted the villa and hurried through the short tunnel and cave that opened into the stunning rock pool. Disrobing, Maisie dived into the pool, submerging for several seconds, hoping the heavenly cool water would wash away her turbulent thoughts.

The strong compulsion to make the most of what she had *now* before it was taken away from her wouldn't dissipate. On the contrary it grew stronger the harder she willed it away, the harder she swam from one end of the pool to the other.

Finally, wrung out emotionally and physically, she perched on the rock beneath the waterfall, leaning her head back to catch the edge of the cascading water, and sighed at the delicious sting of the warm water on her face.

'You insist you have no illusions of pursuing a life as a mermaid, and yet here you are again.'

She jerked at the sound of Romeo's voice and nearly fell into the water. Righting herself, she stared at his imposing, braced-legged stance at the opposite end of the pool. And swallowed hard.

He was dressed, like her, for swimming, his trunks hugging thick, hair-dusted thighs. But whereas she'd worn a tunic, he only wore a towel around his neck. Her breath strangled and died in her lungs, her pulse racing at the sheer magnificence of him.

She was doomed.

She knew it even before he dropped into the pool and swam lazily towards her. Halfway, he ducked under the water, struck out in a powerful crawl and emerged at her feet. Hands braced on either side of her thighs, he stared wordlessly at her, his gaze intense, broodingly ravenous. Maisie stared down at his breathtaking face, the droplets of water glistening on his skin in the moonlight like tiny diamonds.

Raw sexual energy leapt where their skin connected, firing arousal so strong she could almost touch it.

'Did sleep elude you, as it did me, *gattina*?' he enquired with a husky rasp after an endless throb of silence.

She nodded dumbly, her fingers reaching out of their own accord to trace his eyebrow, his cheekbones. His jaw.

'Have you grown tired of fighting the inevitable?' he pressed.

Her blood roared in her ears, drowning out her every resistant thought. 'I've grown tired of fighting you.'

The gleam in his eyes dimmed for a moment. 'It's not me you've been fighting, but yourself. If nothing else, be true to yourself about that, before this goes any further,' he growled, his stare telling her he wouldn't accept anything but her agreement.

And he was right.

She had been fighting this purely for her own self-preservation. How could she not? The consequences should he reject her a second time would be even more devastating than before. She knew it deep in her soul. With the passage of time her feelings towards him were changing, morphing into something deeper, stronger, that she couldn't seem to control.

The movement of the water jerked him a tiny fraction. The result was a slide of her fingers across his hot, beautiful skin, bringing her to the here and now, to the almighty need pounding through her blood.

'I'm tired of fighting,' she whispered raggedly.

'Then surrender,' he urged thickly. 'Just let this be.' His hands moved, sliding over her thighs to capture her knees. Tugging them open, he surged closer, his eyes so fierce and intense they seemed aflame from within. 'I can't stand another night of wanting you and being denied. Of imagining the many ways of having you, without going out of my mind. Surrender, *gattina*. Surrender now.'

Desire, wild and unfettered, wrenched through her, rendering the last of her resistance useless. Her fingers speared into his wet hair, using her hold to tilt his face up to hers.

Bending, she took his mouth in a greedy kiss, intent on gorging herself on a feast she'd stalwartly denied herself but couldn't resist another moment longer.

Somewhere down the line the devastation would be great. When she was back in her role of single mother far away in Ranelagh, her shredded emotions would have time to mourn, to berate her for her choices.

But here...now, in this heavenly place with this man who put the very gods to shame, she would live in the moment. She would just...*live*. As she had that night in Palermo, she would give as much of herself as she could and take what Romeo offered.

She groaned when he moved her closer to the edge of the rock and deepened the kiss, taking over her surrender with the terrifyingly intoxicating thrust of his tongue and the thrilling power of his body.

The waterfall pounded with elemental force behind her, but it was nothing compared to the demanding power of Romeo's kiss. He kissed her as if he'd hungered for her for aeons. As if he couldn't get enough of her.

Being wanted like that was like a drug to her senses. After years of bleak, icy indifference, it was a drug she craved more of with each passing second.

So she protested with a loud whimper when he pulled away. Before she could reach for him, he planted a hand on her belly, pressed her back till she was flat on the rock. He picked up her legs and swung them onto the rock before surging out of the water to join her.

For a long, taut moment, he stared down at her, his gaze

sizzling over her from top to toe. Then he prowled over her, his hands braced on either side of her head.

'I've often imagined you like this, spread over this rock like a pagan sacrifice for me to feast on, to pleasure until neither of us can move. Now here you are, wearing this wisp of clothing meant to tempt even the holiest of saints,' he breathed, triumph blazing through his golden eyes.

'It's a good thing you're not a saint, then, isn't it?' she managed, then watched a wicked smile curl his lips.

'*Sì*, it's a very good thing. Because no saint should be allowed to see you like this. Or allowed to do this.' He flicked his tongue over the wet material of her bikini top, then, with a deep groan, he shoved the material aside with his teeth and repeated the action several times, before pulling her nipple into his mouth.

Her back arched off the rock with a cry that was indeed pagan, thick arousal firing straight between her legs. He suckled long and hard, his groans matching hers as sensation cascaded through her.

'*Dio mio,*' he muttered when he lifted his head. He speared her with an almost shocked expression before he looked down at her exposed breasts. '*Dio mio, gattina*, you're intoxicating. I want to devour every inch of you.' Impatiently, he tugged at the bikini strings, pulling them away to bare her body to him.

A drop of water splashed onto her neglected nipple. With another wicked smile, he licked at it, then trailed his hot mouth down her torso to the line of her bikini bottom. Unable to keep her hands at her sides, Maisie speared her fingers in his hair, holding him to her quivering belly when he nipped her flesh in tiny, erotic bites.

By the time he released the ties and pulled away her meagre covering, she'd skated into pure delirium, compelled by a force beyond her control. She raised her head and met his gaze a second before he tasted the centre of her.

'Oh, God!' The force of her need jerked through her, then

set in motion a series of undulations he was only too glad to follow. When her eyes started to roll shut, he pulled away.

'No, watch me, *gattina*. Watch me enjoy you the way I've been dying to do.'

The eroticism of the request pushed her closer to the edge. Panting, she nodded and kept her gaze on him as he lapped at her, his tongue executing wicked circles that cracked open a previously untapped well of pleasure.

'Romeo,' she groaned raggedly, the rush of feeling almost too much to bear. 'Please…I can't take any more.'

'You can.' Opening her wider, he altered the pressure of his tongue, his hypnotic gaze telling her she was under his control, to do with as he pleased.

When she began to thrash, he simply laid a hand on her belly and continued his assault. And with each kiss, he grew just as possessed with the red-hot fire consuming them.

'Now, Maisie,' he growled against her swollen flesh an eternity later.

With an agonised cry, she let go, her whole body convulsing with a release so powerful, she lost all sense of space and time.

CHAPTER ELEVEN

SHE OPENED HER EYES to find him sprawled next to her, his fingers tracing her mouth as he stared down at her, a peculiar expression simmering in his eyes.

'What?'

He kissed her, her earthy taste on his lips and the reason for it making her blush. When he raised his head, that look still lingered.

'You returned home from Palermo pregnant.' His hand trailed from her neck to her belly and stayed there while his eyes held her prisoner.

'Is there a pointed question in there somewhere?' she murmured, her heartbeat still thundering loud enough to compete with the sound of the waterfall. 'I'm on the Pill now if that's what you're asking. It helps regulate my period.'

'It's not, but that's good to know.' His hand continued to wreak havoc on her. 'You changed careers and forged another life for yourself all alone. Did you at any point seek another man's bed to alleviate your loneliness?' he asked thickly.

She knew how weak and pathetic responding in the positive would make her look. But she couldn't lie. Not when she'd just experienced an incredible earth-moving event.

She threaded her fingers through his wet hair. 'I was alone, not lonely. But no, Romeo. You were the last man I slept with.'

His chest moved in a deep inhalation and his eyes filled once again with that primitive, razor-sharp hunger that threatened to obliterate her.

The hand on her belly trailed to her thighs, his fingers

digging into her skin in an urgent caress as his head dropped to hers once more. Falling into the kiss, Maisie gladly let sensation take over again, moaning when her hand trailed over taut muscle and bone to finally close on his steely length.

She caressed him as he'd once hoarsely instructed her to, a thrill coursing through her when he groaned brokenly against her lips.

All too soon, he was rolling on the condom he'd plucked from his trunks. Bearing her back, he parted her thighs and hooked his arms under her knees.

He stared deep into her eyes and thrust home in one smooth lunge.

'Oh!'

His growl of male satisfaction reverberated to her very soul. Her fingers speared into his hair as he began to pleasure her with long, slow strokes, each one pulling a groan from her that only seemed to turn him on harder.

He kissed her mouth, her throat, her nipples, with a hunger that grew with each penetration, until she was sure he wouldn't stop until she was completely ravished.

'You're mine. Say it,' he demanded gutturally, when her world began to fracture.

'Romeo…'

'I want to hear it, Maisie.' He slid deep and stopped, the harsh, primitive request demanding a response.

Something shifted inside her, a deep and profound knowledge sliding home that once she admitted this there would be no going back. That she would be giving herself over to him completely, body and soul.

He angled his hips, the move a blatant demonstration that he had all the power, that he controlled every fibre of her being.

'I…' She groaned when he moved again, delivering that subtle thrust that sent her to the very edge of consciousness.

'Tell me!'

'I'm yours…yours. Please…' Her nails dug into his back, and she surged up to take his mouth with hers. 'Please, Romeo. I'm yours…take me,' she whispered brokenly.

Romeo moved, his senses roaring from the words, from her tight and wet heat, from the touch of her hands on his skin. He couldn't get enough. He wanted more. All of her, holding absolutely nothing back. He reared back so he could look into her eyes, to see for himself that she meant it, that she belonged to him completely.

Her eyes met his, the raw pleasure coursing through her shining in the stunning blue depths. There was no fight, no holding back, just a beautiful surrender that cracked something hard and heavy in his chest, bringing in the light and abating the tortured, weighted-down bitterness for the first time in his life.

The sense that he could fly free, that he could find even deeper and truer oblivion in her arms than he had their first time in Palermo, slashed across his consciousness, making his thrusts less measured, the need to achieve that transcendental plane a call to his very soul.

He looked down at her, saw her eyes grow dazed and dark as her bliss encroached. Letting go of her legs, he speared his fingers into her hair and kissed her.

'Now, *gattina mia*,' he croaked, knowing he was at the edge of surrender himself.

'Yes, oh, yes,' she replied. Then she was thrashing beneath him, her sex clamping around his in a series of convulsions that sent him over the edge.

With a loud roar, Romeo flew, barely able to keep from crushing her as he found a release so powerful, had he believed in heaven he would've been certain he'd truly found it in that moment.

He came back down to the touch of her hands trailing up and down his back, her mouth moving against his throat in a benediction of soft kisses.

Again another blaze of memory slashed across his mind,

a sense of déjà vu throwing him back five years, to his hotel suite in Palermo. The feeling that he was raw and exposed, that the woman beneath him wasn't one he could bed and discard, pounding through him. Romeo was certain it was why he'd left as he had the next morning, ensuring he left no trace of himself behind.

Because after mere hours with her, he'd instinctively known that Maisie O'Connell had the power to burrow under his skin, unearth tortured truths and hidden desires he wanted no man or woman to unveil. He'd listened abstractedly as she'd spilled her hopes and dreams and had wanted nothing more than to tell her he'd arrived in Palermo the week before, hoping that for once in his life the woman who'd given birth to him would look at him with any feeling other than hate. That he'd spent a week by his mother's bedside, hoping for a morsel of affection, or regret for the way she'd callously discarded him.

He'd somehow managed to keep his tortured thoughts to himself, but he could tell she'd sensed them, and she'd soothed his soul with the same soft kisses and caresses she gifted him with now.

Then, as now, she'd given herself completely, despite not knowing any more than his first name.

The need to unburden completely powered through him now, but he held himself back. She knew about his father partly through the need to furnish her with information about Lorenzo's plans and partly because he'd let down his guard. But his mother was a different story.

The secret shame that clawed through him had never abated, despite the years he'd spent in bitterness. After he'd buried his mother, he'd bricked away the pain, secure in the knowledge that she no longer had the power to hurt him with her rejection. He'd only ever felt those foundations crumble with Maisie. And her power over him wasn't one he felt comfortable with. It spoke to a weakness he wasn't ready to face.

Shoving his unsettling thoughts back in the vault, he stared down and allowed himself to bask in her soft smile. The sex he could more than deal with, even if it came with a brief exposure of his soul. The benefits were worth it. More rewarding than securing the best business deal.

'Should I be afraid of that smug smile you're wearing right now?' she asked, her voice slightly dazed and heavy with spent bliss.

Arousal spiked again, the magic of her body transporting him into pleasure with blinding speed. Replacing the condom, he expertly reversed their positions, lying back to take in her goddess-like beauty.

With her long, wet hair plastered to her golden skin, she truly looked like a wanton mermaid.

'*Sì*, you're about to make another of my fantasies come true.' He cupped her heavy breasts, played his thumbs over the stiff peaks and felt her body quicken to his touch. He grew harder, need lashing through him as he watched her accept, then revel in, her new position.

She tested the rhythm, quickly found one pleasing to them both and commenced a dance that had them gasping and groaning within minutes.

He reached between them and found her heated centre. Playing his fingers expertly over her, he watched her throw back her head, her nails digging into his chest as she screamed her release.

He followed gladly, eager to experience that piece of heaven again. Eager to leave behind hopes and yearnings that would never be fulfilled. He'd refused to wish after seeing each fragile desire turn to dust before his eyes as a child.

But Maisie in his arms, in his bed, was an achievable goal. One he intended to hang on to for as long as he could.

Maisie awoke slowly, her senses grappling with the strange bed she slept in and the warm, solid body tangled around hers. Vague memories of being carried from the waterfall slid through her mind. She stirred and the heaviness of satiation moved through her limbs, bringing back wild and more vivid memories of last night.

Opening her eyes to brilliant sunshine, she forced herself not to panic as the full realisation of what had happened reared up like a giant billboard in front of her.

She'd given herself to Romeo. Not just her body, but her heart, her soul. She'd known right from the start that giving herself to him this time round would be her undoing. Heck, she'd told him as much!

Just as she'd suspected when she'd promised she was his, she'd been making a declaration that went beyond sex. Each decision she'd taken when it came to her child and his father had been made from her heart. She just hadn't been brave enough to admit it to herself. But now she knew.

She was in love with Romeo Brunetti.

Had probably fallen in love with him the moment she'd sat down across from him that day in Palermo.

Her stomach clenched even as her heart accepted the deep, abiding truth. He was the reason she'd never paid another man any attention, had embraced motherhood without much of a thought for finding a father figure for her son. Deep down she'd known no one could come close to Romeo so she hadn't even tried to replace him.

And now… She breathed deep as her eyes fell on her wedding rings. Now, she could do nothing but brace herself for the agony to come. And it would come. Loving Romeo was her greatest risk and would bring the greatest consequence. Of that, she was certain.

'Buon giorno, gattina.' Strong fingers brushed her hair from her face and drew her back against the warm sheets. 'What troubles you so much that you wake me with the power of your thoughts?' he asked, his eyes probing hers with the sharpness of a scalpel.

'Everything and nothing,' she replied obliquely, desperately hoping to buy more time to compose herself.

'An answer guaranteed to send a man into fits of puzzlement. Or the nearest jewellery store.'

'Is that how you usually placate your other women?' she asked, a sensation moving through her that she deciphered as deep jealousy.

Intense eyes narrowed. 'I wasn't aware you needed placating. Perhaps you should tell me where I've misstepped?'

She glanced away. 'I don't. You haven't. Sorry, I was prying again.'

Warm fingers captured her chin, a thoughtful look in his eyes. 'I guess it's only fair, since I questioned you about past liaisons.'

She shook her head, perversely wanting to know, but also desperate to live in denial. If only for a while longer. She chose the latter. 'I don't need a biography of your past conquests. I know enough to get that you have a healthy sexual appetite.' A blush suffused her face and he slanted her a wicked grin.

'Is that what concerns you?'

She shook her head, but she couldn't tell him, of course. Because that would be tantamount to shoving her heart underneath the wheels of a Sherman tank. So she went for the next best thing. 'Why did you bring me to your bedroom? I wasn't expecting to wake up here.'

The smile left his face and that dark brooding look returned. 'Why do you think?' His voice pulsed with an emotion she couldn't name.

She pulled her lower lip into her mouth. 'I thought last night was just…' She paused. 'I meant it when I said I don't want this to get complicated.'

Too late.

But that didn't mean she couldn't salvage a little bit of dignity from the dire situation. Guard her heart from more pulverising down the road.

'So *your* itch has been scratched and you're ready to put

it all behind you?' he queried in a dark, dangerous voice, throwing her own words back in her face.

'I didn't expect it to last beyond last night. Isn't that your record?'

'I see we're back to past conquests again.'

'Romeo—'

'No, you listen. Last night barely dented the depth of my need. And if you're truthful, you'll admit the same. I brought you to my bed because this is where you belong. You can protest as much as you want and we can go back to circling each other until we drive each other insane, or you can choose to admit your feelings and take what you want.'

She opened her mouth, intent on denying everything he'd said. On doing *the right thing*. Getting up, walking back to her own room. To her painfully lonely bed. And more nights filled with the vicious ache of wanting him.

But the words died in her throat. Denying herself suddenly felt like the opposite of *the right thing*. As if saying the words out loud would be like slicing a knife into her arms and opening her veins. Sure, there was a life of desolation waiting for her once she walked away from him, but there was no need to start the torture *now*.

She stared up at him, at the vitality of the body caging hers, the need blazing in his eyes, and resolved to just *be* for now.

'Will you stay?' he pressed.

Slowly, she nodded. 'Yes, I will.'

He proceeded to show her the true meaning of good morning. And she gave herself over to the incandescent sensation.

She was still smiling four mornings later, even as she studiously ignored the tiny voice that called her ten kinds of a fool.

They rose, showered together, their hands and lips revelling in the newness of just being together without tension. Oh, the sexual tension was ever-present. It barely left them alone and Maisie was beginning to doubt it ever would. But there was an ease between them that tugged at her heart when Romeo smiled at her and walked her to her room so she could get dressed.

He lounged in the doorway of her dressing room, his eyes wickedly intent on her body as she pulled on panties and a bra, and slid her white shift dress over her head.

After slipping her feet into heeled sandals, she took his outstretched hand and they left the room.

'Are you sure?' she asked him.

He nodded, although his throat moved in a hard swallow. 'Yes, it's time to tell him.'

As they reached the stairs, she glanced at him and was shocked to see that, for the first time since she'd known him, Romeo looked nervous. Vulnerable.

'Are you okay?' she asked as they descended the stairs and headed towards the kitchen, where Lucca could be heard chattering away to Mahina and Emily.

Romeo gave a strangled laugh. 'It's not every day I tell an almost-four-year-old boy I'm his *papà*.'

Her hand closed on his and drew him to a stop. Standing on tiptoe, she offered what she'd intended to be a supportive kiss.

His hands locked on her hips, and he slammed her back against the wall to deepen the kiss. He kissed her as if trying to draw sustenance from her. By the time they pulled apart several minutes later, they were both breathing hard. His eyes were needy pools, searching and a little lost.

She placed her hand on his cheek, her heart melting when he cupped it and pressed it deeper into his skin. 'You'll be fine. He adores you as much as you do him.'

His head dipped as if he wasn't quite sure how to deal with the alien feeling of being the object of a child's adoration. *'Grazie,'* he finally murmured. When he raised his head, the confident, virile man had slid back. 'Let's do this.'

He tugged her after him, and they entered the kitchen together.

Ten minutes later, in the privacy of Romeo's study, Lucca stared at his father from the safety of his perch on his mother's lap. Then his gaze moved to her face and back to Romeo's, his eyes wide, hazel saucers. 'You're my daddy?' he asked in hushed awe.

Romeo's throat moved several times before he could speak. '*Sì*, I am your *papà*,' he intoned in a deep, moving voice.

Lucca tilted his head to one side, then shook his head. 'Not *papà*...*daddy*. I want you to be a *daddy*.'

A telltale sheen covered Romeo's eyes and he blinked rapidly before he nodded. '*Va bene*, I will be a daddy.'

Lucca launched himself off her lap and threw his arms around his father. Romeo's strong arms gathered the chubby body to him, his eyes closing on a depth of feeling that made Maisie's eyes fill with helpless tears. Father and son stayed locked for an eternity. Or as much as a toddler could stand until impatience set in.

When he was lowered to his feet, Lucca stared up at his father. 'Can I tell Emily?'

Romeo nodded. 'You can tell whomever you wish.'

Lucca started to race out of the door but then stopped suddenly. 'I wished very, very hard for a daddy,' he said solemnly. 'And it came true!'

Romeo looked stricken for several long seconds. Then he shook his head, as if denying whatever thought had crossed his mind. 'I'm glad for you, *bel bambino*.'

After watching Lucca run off, Romeo turned to her and pulled her to her feet. Seeing her tears, he gently wiped them away and planted a soft kiss on her lips. '*Grazie, il mio dolce*.'

Swallowing the lump in her throat, she smiled. 'I told you it'd be a piece of cake,' she said.

His blinding answering smile lit her up from the inside,

starting a shaky weakness that made her lower her gaze in case he read the depth of emotions moving through her. 'Perhaps I should listen to you more,' he suggested with a quirked brow.

'Perhaps I should get that in writing,' she answered.

He was still chuckling when they trailed their son. The announcement turned into an impromptu celebration with pancakes and juice, after which they got down to the urgent business of planning Lucca's heavily duck-pond-themed birthday party.

Finding out that the Giordano family would be joining them on the island in two days, along with the guests staying at the villas, and that Romeo was expected to host a dinner party, Maisie felt a rush of panic.

The only party she'd thrown so far had involved a cake, sandwiches and screaming kids in a playgroup's ball pit.

She was nowhere near sophisticated enough to handle a houseful of billionaires. She tried to pin a smile on her face as Romeo's eyes narrowed at her from across the kitchen island.

'What's wrong?' he asked as soon as they were alone.

'Nothing...' she started to say, then blurted, 'I've never thrown a dinner party before. Or a birthday party for a billionaire's son for that matter.'

He frowned. 'He's still the son you raised from birth. As for the party, everything's taken care of. I have caterers flying in from Honolulu to assist the chefs who cater for the island guests.'

Somehow her anxiety only escalated. 'Oh, so you don't really need me at all, do you?'

His frown deepened. 'Of course I need you. What's this really about?'

On some level, Maisie knew she was reacting to a deeper anxiety, one that stemmed from the knowledge that Romeo's life was so smoothly coordinated, aside from her role in his bed, he didn't need her for much else. Even Lucca would be extremely well taken care of by Emily and Mahina, should Maisie suddenly find herself rubbed out of the picture.

'Maisie?' he growled warningly.

She shrugged. 'I guess I'm feeling a little surplus to re-quirements.' Not to mention suddenly aware of her pre-carious position of temporary wife. 'I barely do anything for Lucca any more besides eat breakfast and sometimes lunch with him. Other times, he'd rather play with Emily or hang out with you.'

He took her by the arms. 'You've had him to yourself for almost four years. It's understandable the small sepa-ration on occasion would feel strange. And that separation was probably more pronounced because you were avoid-ing *me*,' he pointed out. 'But if you want me to prove that you're not surplus to requirements, just say the word, and I'll oblige you.'

She looked into eyes darkening into burnished gold and a blaze sparked through her. But alongside it rose a wave of desolation. Sex with Romeo was out of this world. Each experience felt as if she were touching the stars. But it was *just sex* for him. It would never be anything more.

So when he gathered her close and kissed her, she re-sponded with a lingering taste of sadness that made tears brim behind her closed eyes.

His phone rang just when she thought the tears would spill and betray her, and she breathed a sigh of relief. He pulled it from his pocket and checked the screen. Frown-ing, he looked at her. 'Sorry, it's Zaccheo. I have to take it.'

Waving him away, she hurriedly escaped the sunlit liv-ing room. Her first thought was to find Lucca. She found him in the playroom and pulled him into a close em-brace. When he demanded she read his favourite story, she obliged.

She was on the fifth read when Romeo entered the room.

She jerked upright at the volcanic fury on his face. 'What's wrong?'

'Zaccheo and Eva are arriving tomorrow.'

A day earlier than planned. 'Why?'

'Because they've been pulled into this insane situation in Palermo. It's time to end this before it gets out of hand.'

CHAPTER TWELVE

HER FIRST IMPRESSION of Zaccheo Giordano drove home the understanding of why the two powerful men were friends.

He carried himself with the same ruthless energy as Romeo, albeit with a little less brooding intensity. That energy was exhibited clearly when he stepped from the buggy and clasped Romeo's hand in an unsmiling, yet moving greeting.

His intensity lessened dramatically when he helped his heavily pregnant wife up the short steps into the wide villa entranceway.

Eva Giordano was gorgeous in a pocket-Venus, burst-of-energy way that drew interested eyes to her wild tumble of blonde hair and sharply contrasting dark eyebrows and darkly ringed green eyes.

Despite the strong evidence of love between them, Maisie sensed a tension between her and Zaccheo, which was explained once introductions had been made and Romeo was hugging Eva.

'I'm sorry we had to descend on you prematurely, but it was either *we all* came here or *we all* went to Palermo.' She cast an irritated look at her husband. 'The vote was eventually unanimous that we come here, since I refused to be left behind while Caveman over here went off to tackle Carmelo and Lorenzo on his own.'

Zaccheo muttered under his breath about intransigent women and helped corral his twin sons when they escaped their nanny and started fighting over who was better suited to drive the buggy.

Eva turned from greeting Romeo and her gaze fell on

Lucca. 'Oh, hello there, beautiful boy.' Her wide smile seemed to enchant her husband, who lost his growly look and came to stand beside her, one hand gently caressing her swollen belly.

The look of pure, blazing love that passed between them caused Maisie's heart to drop in misery into her belly. But she managed a smile and coaxed a shy Lucca from behind her. Within minutes he and the Giordano boys were exploring the new toy room Romeo had installed for him.

Mahina served drinks on the terrace and the tension mounted again the moment she left.

'What exactly did Carmelo want from you?' Romeo asked tersely, once Zaccheo had apprised them of the threat from Palermo's other crime lord.

'His ridiculous demands are the same as Lorenzo's to you. They're both terrified one would attain more power than the other. But he had the nerve to threaten my family. I cannot allow that to stand.'

Eva rolled her eyes. 'You realise how much like a bad gangster movie actor you sound?' When his eyes narrowed, she continued, completely unfazed. 'You have a veritable army guarding me and the boys when you're not around, and Carmelo's claims of you owing him allegiance because your father was a one-time lieutenant of his before he switched sides to Romeo's father is flimsy at best. How do we even know that's true?' She looked at Romeo. 'Besides, I know you two have enough dirt on the man to send him to jail for a long time.'

Romeo shook his head. 'I've talked to the lawyers about it. It's all circumstantial without hard evidence. I only witnessed Zaccheo's father being beaten.' He sent his friend a look of grim-faced sympathy, to which Zaccheo nodded. 'He was still alive when I was thrown out of Fattore's mansion. We need irrefutable evidence of blood on Lorenzo's hands.'

'So, what's the alternative?' Eva exclaimed. 'A duel at dawn beneath Mount Etna?'

Romeo's jaw clenched but he didn't refute Eva's outlandish claim. Maisie's stomach hollowed out, both at the news Romeo had just delivered and his intent expression.

'You're not thinking of going back to Palermo, are you?' she demanded in a shocked whisper.

His eyes when they met hers were hard, implacable, with no trace of the gentleness they'd held yesterday before Zaccheo's phone call. 'It's the only option. I won't entertain the idea of my son living in fear.'

Zaccheo nodded in grim agreement and captured his wife's hand when she began to protest.

Maisie struggled not to feel excluded and even more miserable as Romeo proceeded to converse to the couple, switching to Italian when the debate got heated.

Once or twice, she spotted Eva's probing glance and fixed a smile on her face, answering her questions about the island and the villa when she switched back to English.

When Eva yawned loudly and started to droop, Zaccheo stood and ushered her inside.

Knowing she wouldn't be able to sit and make small talk while her insides were shredding with the knowledge that Romeo had room in his heart only for his son, and not her, she jumped to her feet.

'I'll go see if the boys are okay.'

He caught her hand and stopped her. 'You're upset because I intend to confront Lorenzo?'

'Does my opinion matter enough for you to change your mind? I thought you were pursuing a different route other than direct confrontation.'

His jaw flexed. 'I suspected his mellowed stance was all a bluff. Just as I suspect, this is nothing more than an extortion scheme, probably concocted between him and Carmelo. The timing is a little too synchronised. Whatever it is, I need to end it once and for all.'

She tried to pull away but he held on. 'Since your mind's made up, there's no need for my opinion, is there?'

'Gattina—'

'Don't call me that.' The blurted plea rushed out before she could stop it.

He gave a hiss of frustration. 'You suddenly have a problem with the name?'

'No, only your use of it when you're trying to put me back in your little box marked *Handled.*'

His mouth twisted. 'Even if such a box existed, the physical and psychological scratch marks you leave on me would point to an abject failure in my task.'

She tugged at her hand again until he freed her. 'And you'll continue to fail. Because I won't be put in a box and labelled as to what I need to be. Never again.'

A new tension stilled his body. 'You think that's what I've been doing to you?'

'What have you been doing, if not knocking down my every objection in a bid to get your way since you found out about Lucca?' she threw back.

'He's my son. There was never a doubt that I would claim him. You knew that. Did you think I wouldn't do everything in my power to give him everything that had been denied me?' he demanded.

'No, but what sort of mother would I have been if I'd wilfully turned my back on the one thing you led me to believe would save our son.'

His nostrils flared. 'You believe that's no longer true?'

'I went along with this marriage because it would protect us while you found a *business* solution to this problem. Now you tell me you're planning some sort of vendetta-settling and I'm left asking myself whether this marriage was worth the aggravation I put myself through in the first place if the outcome is going to be a different one! Would I not have been better off in Ranelagh, alone with my son while you carelessly diced with death?'

A searing wave of shock washed over his face before his eyes, mouth and jaw hardened in a look of pure bitterness.

'So you regret this marriage?' he demanded in a low, icy voice.

'Tell me the truth, Romeo. Was marrying me really necessary?'

His jaw clenched for a long time before he bit out, 'Yes.'

'To save Lucca from Lorenzo or to give him your name?'

Her heart threatened to beat itself out of existence, and her limbs felt frozen and useless as she stared at him.

'At the time, the two weren't mutually exclusive.'

'So you didn't exaggerate one to get the other?'

He jerked upright and strode to the edge of the terrace, his movements erratic. For several minutes he said nothing, and slowly his balled fists loosened.

Then he turned. 'You're right. I should've thought this through a little longer, given myself better options.'

Maisie's agonised gasp was barely audible, but it seemed to open a new set of floodgates, bringing fresh waves of pain. She knew she was a fool then for expecting him to tell her their marriage wasn't a mistake. That it was more than just a means to ensure Lucca's safety. That however it'd started out, it was worth holding on to, worth salvaging.

Hearing his words brought home to her just how foolish she'd been to hope. Just like five years ago, Romeo had made a mistake with her. One he regretted. Only this time, he'd told her so to her face rather than let his absence speak for him.

Footsteps preceded Zaccheo's reappearance on the terrace and brought a jagged but final end to the conversation. Catching the other man's narrow-eyed, assessing glance, she pinned a smile on her face. 'I'm going to check on the boys.'

She stumbled blindly indoors, operating on automatic rather than with any sense of purpose, as she headed for the toy room. Reaching the doorway, she saw that Emily and the Giordano nanny had readied the boys for bed.

Forcing her feet to move, she went to her son and brushed her fingers over his hair. He looked up for a moment, his deep hazel eyes connecting with hers in a wide, loving look before he was distracted by one of his new best friends.

Feeling lost, cast adrift in a merciless ocean, Maisie wandered back out, trying hard not to buckle under the realisation that she'd sped up her exit from Romeo's life with that last tirade. Because surely telling the man who'd married you for the sake of his son that you'd rather not be married to him was a request to be freed the moment the necessity became obsolete?

Pain ripped through her heart as she entered her bedroom. How could it look so bleak and lonely after just a few short nights spent away from it? How could her heart shred so badly at the thought that she wouldn't spend another night in Romeo's bed?

A broken moan, much like a manifestation of grief, poured out of her throat as she sank onto the side of her bed.

Her shame at the knowledge that she would shed her dignity for another night in Romeo's bed bit deep as she lay back and sobbed into her pillow. She would go back on her word, on the promise she'd made after distancing herself from her parents' continued disapproval never to contort herself into another's expectations of her. She would put herself in a box labelled *desperate and willing to beg for Romeo's love* if she had the faintest glimpse that he returned a sliver of what she felt for him.

The sickening feeling of how far she would go triggered harder sobs, until her head throbbed and her body was wrung out. Still the pain came, washing over her in waves as the sun slid low and she knew she had to get up and dress for dinner.

Over and over as she showered, she saw his face, felt his silence like a final, doomed slash across her heart and wondered how she would face him across the dinner table. For a moment she wished for the man who had brushed her feelings aside and taken control. But she shook her head.

They'd gone past that this afternoon. There was no hiding from the glaring knowledge that Romeo didn't love her and never would. That his only interest was for his son.

Her only choice was to muddle through the next few days, and leave the island when Romeo did. If he was intent on having his son guarded by a security detail, he could do so in Ranelagh. She wouldn't be able to bear staying here, cocooned in a fool's paradise. She would confront reality head-on, put one foot in front of the other until she learned to live with the pain.

Shutting off the shower, she dressed in an ensemble appropriate for entertainment, applied enough make-up to disguise the puffiness under her eyes and left her room.

She encountered Eva emerging from her own suite and pinned a smile on her face.

'Oh, good, were you going to check on Lucca? We can share story time and be done in half the time,' Eva said with an engaging grin.

They entered the large guest suite where the children had been relocated after Lucca refused to be parted from his new friends and took turns reading until all three fell asleep.

In the living room, they found the men sipping whiskies. Romeo crossed to the drinks cabinet and returned with a mineral water for Eva and a glass of champagne for her, which he handed over with a rigidly blank look on his face.

Her breath caught painfully and she looked away as Eva smiled and patted the bump covered by her stunning jade-green gown. 'Sorry I conked out on you earlier. These two kept me up during the flight with their incessant kicking.'

Maisie's eyes widened. 'You're having another set of twins?'

Eva grinned. 'Turns out twins run in both our families. My great-grandmother was a twin, and Zaccheo's mother told him his grandfather was a twin, too. Something to be thankful for, since he's determined to not stop knocking me up until he has a full football team. That means I get to do this *only* half a dozen times.'

Zaccheo broke off his muffled conversation with Romeo and strolled over to his wife. 'You know you love carrying my children, *dolcezza*.'

'Yeah, keep telling yourself that, champ. After these two I'm taking an extended leave of absence from getting pregnant.'

Zaccheo lifted a brow. 'As long as it's merely a leave and not a resignation.'

Eva rolled her eyes but curled into his side when he sat down next to her.

The conversation turned to children. Romeo maintained brooding silence throughout, and only offered brusque opinions when Eva forced him into the conversation. Zaccheo seemed perfectly at ease with Romeo's mood, but Maisie couldn't help her breath catching whenever Romeo slid her an icy glance.

The tense atmosphere continued through dinner, the men chatting about business and Eva attempting to engage Maisie in general conversation. She couldn't remember because she was concentrating on keeping the sob at the back of her throat whenever she looked at Romeo.

And how pathetic was that? To know she'd been nothing more than a plaything in his bed while he got to know his son, and yet still feel as if her world were caving in on itself every time she remembered that in a handful of days she would walk away from him for ever.

'Oh, for goodness' sake. Can we sort this thing out once and for all? Can't you see how distressed this is all making Maisie?'

Her head jerked up at Eva's sharp retort to find the other woman glaring at her husband.

Zaccheo turned to her with one brow tilted. 'Don't get yourself worked up, *dolcezza*. Everything's under control.'

Eva snorted. 'God, you men can be so blind at times! Can't you see we're tearing ourselves apart here? Tell them, Maisie.'

Both sets of male eyes turned towards her, one grimly amused and the other as icily brooding as they'd been all evening.

Painfully pulling her gaze from Romeo's, she pursed her lips. 'Sorry, it seems I no longer have a vote.' Not that she ever did. Or ever would.

Eva sighed heavily and pulled her fingers through her wild, curly blonde hair. 'What do we have to do to get through to you two?' she demanded, exasperated.

'Eva, *mia*, I won't have you this distressed,' Zaccheo all but growled.

'Then stop this stupid cavemen course of action.' She threw her napkin down, winced when her babies also made their thoughts known about the effect her distress was having on them. Zaccheo started to rise, but she waved him away. 'I'm fine. I think Maisie and I will go for a walk, leave you two to ponder the wisdom of your ideas.'

The excuse to be out of Romeo's oppressive presence was too great to turn down. Rising, she took the arm Eva held out after kicking off her shoes. Following her, Maisie kicked off her shoes, too, and they headed outside.

'I hear there's a stunning waterfall here somewhere. I'd love to see it.'

Maisie stumbled to a halt. 'Um…do you mind if we don't?' she pleaded raggedly, unable to bear the thought of returning to where she and Romeo had made love. She knew she'd given herself away when Eva's eyes widened.

'Of course,' she murmured softly. 'We'll go down to the beach instead.'

They walked in silence for a while, taking in the lush vegetation gleaming under strung-out lights, and the view of a night-lit Maui in the distance, before Eva glanced at her. 'You'll have to take the bull by the horns at some point, you know. Men are obtusely blind sometimes—even the cleverest, billion-dollar-empire-commanding ones can fail to see what's right in front of their faces.'

Maisie shook her head. 'It's not like that between Romeo and me,' she painfully explained.

'Maybe not, but the pain you are feeling right now, I've been there. It took weeks before I came to my senses, and I didn't have a toddler to contend with during that time. You and Romeo—there's something there.' She stopped Maisie when she opened her mouth to deny it. 'You had his child four years ago, and he married you within two days of seeing you again.'

'Because of Lucca.'

Eva pursed her lips. 'I married Zaccheo because I thought I didn't have a choice. But deep down, I knew I did. Things happen for a reason, but it's the endgame that matters. Fighting for what you want even when you think everything's hopeless.'

'I don't *think* it's hopeless. I know it is,' she stressed.

Eva looked as if she wanted to argue the point, but her lashes swept over her lovely green eyes and she nodded. 'Okay. I'm sorry for prying. I'll let the matter drop, except to say I've never seen Romeo like this before. Sure, he has that sexy brooding thing going on most of the time, but never like this, not even five years ago, when his mo—' She stopped, visibly pursing her lips to prevent her indiscretion.

Maisie's chest tightened. 'Something bad happened to bring him to Palermo then, didn't it?' It went to show how much she didn't know about Romeo.

'I can only say a bad chapter of his life came to an end. But he wasn't as affected as he is now.'

Maisie shook her head. 'This is all about Lucca,' she insisted as they reached the beach.

Eva nodded, a sage smile curving her lips, before she pulled up the skirt to her elegant gown. 'Okay. Now I'm probably going to ruin my dress, but since my husband refuses to allow me to swim in the ocean until our sons are born, but he happens to be annoying me a lot right now, I'm damn well going for a quick dip.'

Maisie gave a smile that barely lifted the corners of her mouth. 'You know he can see you from the villa, right?'

Eva gave a stubborn, cheeky smile. 'I'll be out before he gets here.'

Maisie didn't think it was wise to stand in her way. The waters weren't especially deep for half a mile or so, but she kept an eye on her, trying not to think about what Eva had said.

Because it wasn't a subject worth pursuing. Romeo had made himself more than clear. And if he'd looked shocked, it was because he probably hadn't thought she would confront him about it.

After a few minutes, tired of the agony replaying through her soul, Maisie adjusted her clothing and waded into the warm, inviting water.

CHAPTER THIRTEEN

ROMEO DIDN'T LOOK UP from the fireplace when his friend joined him, but he accepted the glass containing a double shot of whisky Zaccheo held out to him.

'Tell me your wife drives you half as crazy as mine does me,' Zaccheo growled.

Romeo downed half the glass's content and stared into the remaining amber liquid. 'She's not my wife,' he growled.

'That ring on your finger and the misery on your face tell a different story, *mio fratello*,' Zaccheo challenged with a grim chuckle.

Romeo's chest squeezed at the term. Although he'd only connected with Zaccheo for a brief month when they were children, he'd never forgotten the boy whose life had touched his. Rediscovering that bond of brotherhood as an adult had made Romeo believe he wasn't truly alone in this world. But lately, he'd discovered there were various forms of loneliness.

A loneliness of the heart, for instance…

Zaccheo's hand of friendship might have conquered a small part of his soul, but he was finding out, much to his emerging horror, that it would never be enough. Not like what he'd been secretly hoping for a few weeks.

'The ring is meaningless. She doesn't want to be married to me,' he snapped and downed the rest of the drink. A replacement arrived seconds later, and he took it, his fingers tightening around the cold glass. The platinum-and-gold wedding ring in question caught the light, winking mockingly, and a deep urge to smash the glass moved through him.

Before he could give in to it, Zaccheo replied, 'Before you tear the place to pieces, perhaps you should listen to what your woman has to say.'

'She's already said her piece. And I heard her loud and clear.' Although he wished he hadn't. He wished he hadn't stopped her on the terrace in the first place, that he'd postponed the moment of complete rejection for a while longer.

Why? So he could continue to live in this fool's paradise?

'I've learned to my cost that there's a difference between listening and hearing.'

Romeo's mouth twisted. 'You sound like a damn agony-aunt talk-show host. A very bad one.'

'Mock all you want. You'll learn the difference soon enough.'

Used to Zaccheo providing solid, formidable opinions when needed, Romeo wondered whether his friend was going soft in the head. A glance at him as he strolled to the window to look down at the beach where his wife and Maisie had headed proved otherwise. The ruthless man was behind those strong features.

Zaccheo turned towards him. 'What are we going to do about Palermo? We need to resolve it soon before my wife decides she doesn't want to be married to me any more, either.' The mocking tone belied the brutal intent in his face.

Romeo shook his head. 'Fattore's absurd demands started all of this. Eva's right. You need to be with her and the boys in New York. I'll handle Lorenzo and Carmelo.'

The old man was what had set all this in motion. And while he was grateful for having his son in his life, he couldn't let the nuisance carry on any longer.

The need to teach Fattore's ex-lieutenant a salutary lesson charged through him and he rolled his tense shoulders. 'I should've gone with my instincts and cut Lorenzo off at the knees much sooner, instead of entertaining his foolishness.'

'You needed time to find out what he was capable of.'

'And now I have.'

His phone buzzed and he looked at the screen. Speak of the devil.

'Lorenzo.' His blood boiled as he put his phone on speaker. 'You've saved me the trouble of a phone call.'

'*Bene*. You have good news for me, I hope.'

'I don't deal in hope, old man. Never have,' Romeo snarled.

Zaccheo gave a grim smile and sipped his whisky.

'Whether you like it or not, you have blood ties to this family. Your father left it to you. You can't just turn your back on it.'

Romeo exhaled through the need to punch something. He managed to suppress his rage and frustration and glanced at Zaccheo.

The man he considered his only friend also wore an expression of quiet rage. Romeo knew Zaccheo had learned a thing or two about seeking retribution from his wrongful imprisonment several years ago. Just as he knew the threat against his sons would need to be answered.

But he also knew getting dragged into a Mafia war wasn't what either of them wanted. What he wanted was to be done with this in a single, definitive way.

He hardened his voice so there would be no mistaking his intent.

'You've insisted on shoving my parentage down my throat every chance you got to suit your needs. Well, you got your wish. I'll be in Palermo in seventy-two hours. I promise, you won't like the news I deliver.'

He ended the call and threw the phone on the sofa. About to down his drink, he noticed Zaccheo's rising tension as he stared at the beach far below. In a split second, his friend's disbelieving expression turned into bewilderment. '*Madre di Dio*, is that…? Are they…?'

Romeo followed his gaze, and horror swept through him. 'Yes, they're swimming in the ocean,' he supplied grimly.

And Maisie was further out, almost at the point where the ocean floor dipped dangerously.

'*Porca miseria*, only my wife would decide to swim in the Pacific Ocean fully clothed and at five months pregnant with twins.' He sprinted towards the door with Romeo fast on his heels.

They reached the beach in minutes, with Zaccheo a few feet ahead of him, just as Eva waded ashore. Romeo didn't have to guess that she was exhausted, despite the sheer exhilaration on her face.

Exhilaration that turned into wary apprehension when she spotted her husband's thunderous look. She put out her hands. 'Zaccheo—'

'Not a single word, *dolcezza*, if you know what's good for you,' he sliced at her, before scooping her into his arms and striding off the beach.

Romeo rushed past them, toeing off his socks and shoes. He'd discarded his jacket and shirt as they raced from the villa. He dived into the water, striking out for the lone figure a quarter of a mile away.

He reached Maisie in minutes. And she had the audacity to look at him with a puzzled expression.

'What are you doing out here? Is Eva all right?' she asked.

'What the hell do you think you're doing?' he snapped.

'I thought it was obvious.' She searched the beach, her face turning anxious. 'Is—'

'*Sì*, Eva is fine,' he reassured impatiently. 'Although I've no idea what she was thinking, going for a swim in her condition.'

'She's a strong swimmer, and I was right beside her until she decided to head back. Then I made sure I kept an eye on her.'

'From here, close to where the currents swirl dangerously?' he accused. He couldn't see below the water, but he could see the neckline of her gown and knew how long her dress was, and how hopelessly inept she would've been at saving herself had she been caught in a rip current.

Her mouth twisted as she treaded water. 'Did I not mention I was regional champion swimmer? It was one of the many *almost* talents my parents tried and failed to turn me into. Sadly, I never made it to nationals. One of my many, *many* failures, I guess.' The bitterness in her voice caught him in the raw, threatened to rip open a place he didn't want touched. Especially not since her declaration this afternoon.

'So you thought you'd add one more tick to this imaginary quota by wearing a dress that adds at least twenty pounds to your body weight when it's soaking wet?' he snarled, all the alien feelings that had been bubbling through him since their conversation on the terrace this afternoon rising to the edge.

She looked away from him, and he could've sworn she blushed before her face tightened with deep unhappiness. 'Not exactly.'

He caught hold of her shoulders and pointed her towards the beach. 'Swim back now.'

Her chin rose mutinously. 'Or what?'

Despite the dark emotions swirling through him...the searing agony of knowing that ultimately this woman didn't want him, the knife-edge of arousal lanced him at the fire in her eyes. 'You swim back under your own steam or I drag you back. Those are the only two choices available to you.'

'Romeo—'

'Now,' he interrupted her, unable to believe how like heaven and how very much like hell it felt to hear his name on her lips. 'You may be in a hurry to end this marriage, but it won't be through you carelessly drowning yourself.'

Her mouth dropped open in stunned shock, and he wanted to believe tears filled her eyes, but she turned abruptly and struck out towards shore before he could be certain, her strokes surprisingly swift and strong considering what she wore. He waited until she was a few dozen feet away before he followed.

She was wading waist deep by the time he passed her a few metres from shore. Heading for the cabana where fresh supplies of towels were stocked, he grabbed two and stalked back.

'You had no right to say that to me!'

Romeo looked up and stopped dead. 'What the hell are you wearing? Where's the rest of your dress? And I had no right to say what?' he tagged on abstractedly, unable to tear his eyes away from her body.

'To say that I'd deliberately drown myself.'

'I didn't say you'd do it deliberately, but I didn't think you'd be that careless, either. Although from the look of you, I was wrong in my assumption.'

The bottom part of her dress was missing, leaving her clad in a scrap of wet white lace that brought a growl straining from his chest. And with the top part wet and plastered to her skin, Romeo wondered how long he would last on his own two feet before the strength of need pounding through him buckled his knees.

Under the lights strung out between the palm trees, he watched heat crawl up her face. Although it was a fraction of the fire lighting through his veins. 'Care to tell me what happened to the rest of your dress?' he asked, his voice thick and alien to his own ears.

She waved at the sand near the steps. 'The skirt's over there. The top and bottom are joined by a zip,' she supplied. 'See, I wasn't as stupid as you imagined,' she added bitterly. 'Nor did I plan on risking drowning, either accidentally or deliberately. Amongst other things, I love my son too much to do that.'

Romeo wanted to ask what those other things were, whether it could include him, but for the first time in his life he stepped back from the need to know, his mind clasping on the fact that she hadn't corrected him on the need to end their marriage. Weariness moved through him, parts of him he didn't want to acknowledge feeling brutalised, as if he'd gone ten rounds with an unseen opponent and emerged the loser.

'Are you going to stand there all night or will you hand me one of those towels?' she asked in a low, tense voice.

He started to hand it to her, then stopped. Moving closer, he stared into her eyes, darker now with whatever emotions swirled through her. 'You're not a failure.'

'What?' she croaked, her face raised to his.

'In the water, you said you'd failed at many things.'

'Oh.' Her eyes darkened further and tears brimmed her eyes. 'I have. I failed to get my parents to love me, for instance.'

Her naked pain slashed him hard, despite thinking he'd steeled himself adequately against further unsettling emotion. 'That is *their* fault, not yours. I've learned the hard way that, with the best will in the world, you can't get someone to love you if they're incapable of it.'

Her eyes widened, questions swimming in her eyes. Questions he felt too raw to answer right then. He shook his head and briskly rubbed the towel in her hair. 'You're a huge success at the things you're passionate about.'

Her eyelids swept down, hiding her expression from him. Her laugh was hollow as she tried to take the towel from him. 'I wish I could agree, but sadly the evidence states otherwise. For one thing, you insist on calling what we have a marriage, but has it really been? Or have I just been the body to warm your bed while you burrow your way into your son's life? The woman you didn't trust enough to let her know how much legitimising your son means to you.'

His arms dropped. 'Maisie—'

'Don't, Romeo. I don't want to hear your slick excuses. The moment you found out about Lucca, you wanted him, regardless of who stood in your way. You scooped me up for the ride because that was the easiest option for you.'

He stepped behind her, and his gaze was dragged help-lessly over her body, down the enticing line of her spine to the twin dimples at the top of her buttocks, and the allur-ing globes below, perfectly framed by the wet lace caress-ing her skin.

'Easy? You think any of this has been easy?' He shook his head in self-disgust. 'I'm stumbling round in the dark, pretending I've got my head screwed on straight when the reality is that I'm terrified I'll irrevocably mess up a four-year-old boy's life. And, believe me, I'm perfectly equipped to do it. Whereas you know the answer to every question he asks. You know what he wants before he does. So yes, I exploited your devotion to him to help me get to know my flesh and blood. Condemn me for that, but believe me, *none* of this has been easy for me,' he rasped.

Her head fell forward with a defeated sigh. He told him-self to remember that she intended to walk away, take away the only thing resembling a true family he'd ever known. She was the reason he couldn't take a full breath without wondering if his organs were functioning properly. Some-how, she'd taught him to hope again, to dare to dream. And she'd smashed that dream with a handful of words.

Romeo *tried* to remember that.

But he couldn't help it. He lowered his head and brushed his lips against the top of her spine, where the wet hair had parted to reveal her creamy skin.

She made a sound, part arousal, part wary animal, but he was too far gone to heed the latter. The thought of her leaving, of never being able to do this again, scattered his thoughts to a million pieces, until only one thing mattered.

Here and now.

'Maisie.' He heard the rough plea in his voice. He dropped the towel and trailed his mouth over her shoul-ders, down her back, anxiety hurrying his movements. She shuddered under his touch.

'Romeo, please…'

He dropped to his knees and spun her around. '*Tesoro mio*, don't deny me this. Don't deny *us* this.' He wanted to say more, bare himself with words that were locked deep, but it was as if the language he needed to express himself was suddenly alien to him. But he could show her. He *would* show her.

He held her hips and kissed her soft belly, where his son had nestled, warm and loved. She gave a soft moan. Empowered, he deepened the caress, his tongue tasting her intoxicating skin. When she swayed and her hands clutched his shoulders, he groaned.

Roughly pulling her panties to one side, he fastened his mouth to her sex, caressing her with his tongue as he lapped at her.

'Romeo!'

He drowned beneath the heady sensation, of his wildcat digging her fingers into his skin. He dared to entertain the thought that there might be a way through this landmine that threatened to destabilise his world. He went harder, desperate to bring her pleasure, unashamed to hope it brought him something *more*, something lasting.

She gave another cry and shattered in his arms, her head dropping forward as she shuddered. Rising, he caught her in his arms, saw the dazed but almost resigned look in her eyes, and his stomach hollowed.

Ignoring the look, he carried her to the steps and helped her with the skirt. Then, covering her top half with the towel, he swung her into his arms and headed for the villa.

'I can walk, Romeo,' she said in a small, tight voice.

'I believe I'm living up to my caveman reputation.'

'You're performing to the wrong audience. You don't need to prove anything to me.'

He glanced down at her tear-stained face and his chest tightened. 'Do I not?'

She shook her head, but her eyes refused to meet his. 'I think we understand each other perfectly.'

He wanted to rail at her that he didn't understand; that he'd thought their moment at the waterfall, *before* they'd made love, had started something they could build on. Her mutinous expression stopped him.

Besides, he was beginning to think they communicated much better using a different language.

Entering the villa, he headed for the stairs and his bedroom. The moment she raised her head and looked around, she scrambled from his arms.

Romeo set her down and shut the door.

'Why have you brought me here?' she demanded.

The accusation in her eyes ripped through him but he forced himself not to react to it. Reaching for the towel, he tugged it from her, then he pulled her close.

'Answer me, Romeo…'

'Shh, *gattina*, just let this be.' Another rough plea he was unashamed of, even though it threw him back to another time, another place, pleading in a much younger but equally desperate voice.

It was the night his mother had packed his meagre belongings in a tattered bag and told him she was sending him to his thug of a father.

Disturbed by the memories that seemed intent on flooding in, he sealed his mouth to Maisie's, searching for her unique balm that soothed his soul.

His heart leapt when she didn't push him away, but then she wasn't responding, either. Groaning in frustration, he pushed his fingers into her hair, desperate to stem the alarm rising through him that he was fighting a losing battle.

Eventually, she tore her mouth away. 'Please stop. I don't want this.'

He raised his head, the landmine seeming to spread like an ocean before him. 'This?' he intoned starkly.

Her eyes slid past his, to a point beyond his shoulder. 'You. I don't want you.'

Acrid bitterness filled him, along with the sharp barbs

of memory, but still he pushed. 'That's a lie. I proved it once, I can prove it again and as many times as you need to face the truth.'

She shook her head wearily. 'That was just the sex talking. Nothing more.'

'So you mean you don't want me, the man?' Why did that feel so damn agonising to say?

Her gaze remained averted for another minute before meeting his eyes. 'You're an amazing father, and I'm sure you'll offer Lucca support and opportunities in life I can only dream of. But I can't stay with you. After our guests leave, I'm returning to Ireland with Lucca. I'm sorry, but this…this was a mistake.'

She started to take her rings off. He lunged for her hands, stopped the action before he fully realised he'd moved. 'You will not take off your ring!' The snarled command stemmed from deep within his soul.

Her blue eyes reflected pain, enough to hammer home just how much being here, being with him, was costing her. How could he not have seen that? How could he have entertained the idea that they could attempt a proper marriage?

'I can't…'

'I know my opinion matters very little to you, but think of our son. It's his birthday tomorrow. Are you this determined to throw a shadow over the occasion?'

Her face lost a trace of colour. 'Of course not.'

'Then wait. For his sake.'

Her head dipped and she pushed the rings slowly back on her finger. He forced himself to drop her hands, move away.

'I'll see you in the morning,' she murmured.

He didn't respond. He was struggling to find even the simplest explanation of what was going on inside him. He heard the door shut and paced to the window. In the reflection behind him, he saw the bed they'd risen from this morning and wondered at how much he hated the idea of sleeping in it now.

Undressing, he entered the shower and let the water beat over his head. It wouldn't drown out her words, her face.

I can't stay with you.

His bitter laughter rose above the pounding cascade.

At least those words had been less harsh than the ones his mother had thrown at him before she'd left him on Agostino Fattore's doorstep.

At least this time he wouldn't starve. Or live rough.

And yet he found himself bypassing the bed when he left the bathroom, and collapsing onto the sofa in his private living room. And when he was still awake when the orange streaked the horizon, he'd almost convinced himself the pain ripping through him wasn't worse than it'd been when he was a child.

The performance Maisie gave the next day was award-worthy. At some point while she was smiling and taking pictures of her son at what had been dubbed *The Best Birthday Party Ever*, she half hysterically toyed with contacting her parents and telling them they should've tried enrolling her into acting school.

Because she was able to stand next to Romeo as he helped an ecstatic Lucca cut the ribbon that officially unveiled his duck pond. Then look into his eyes and smile as they helped their son release the fifty balloons tied to the sturdy bridge in the middle of the pond. She even managed a laugh as two necking swans were immediately named Maisie and Romeo. She didn't crumble into a pain-ravaged heap when Lucca insisted his father kiss his mother to celebrate the naming.

And she certainly aced the small talk with the grown-ups while the kids took turns at the duck-feed dispenser.

Once the birthday-cake candles had been blown, the cake devoured, the children tucked in bed, she retired to her suite, showered and got ready for the dinner party.

She stood by Romeo's side as they greeted the two couples Romeo had trusted to remain on the island. Then calling on her skills as a restaurant owner, she supervised the caterers, made sure each guest was looked after, while avoiding being too close to Romeo for longer than a few minutes.

Luckily, Eva, and the phenomenon of carrying a second set of twins, quickly became the centre of attention and, seeming to have made up with her husband, engaged everyone with her effervescent personality.

As soon as the last guest left, Maisie headed for the door.

Romeo blocked her path. She stopped, her heart pounding.

'Well done on the dinner party,' he muttered.

She tried to avert her gaze, to stop absorbing every expression and contour of his face. But she couldn't look away.

'Thank you,' she replied.

He stared at her for another long moment, then he stepped away. 'Goodnight.'

She couldn't respond because her heart had lodged itself in her throat. Hurrying away, she gave in to the insane urge to glance over her shoulder. Romeo was watching her.

She tried to tell herself she didn't yearn for him to follow. By the time she got to her room and shut the door behind her, she knew she was lying to herself.

CHAPTER FOURTEEN

THEY LEFT THE ISLAND two days later, with a distraught Lucca heartbroken at having to leave his beloved ducks. Although he was slightly appeased at the thought of returning to his old pond at Ranelagh Gardens, Maisie knew there would be more tears when he found out his father wouldn't be staying.

The thought troubled her as she played with Lucca during the long flight. A couple of times, she'd attempted to start a conversation with Romeo about scheduling visits, but he'd given her a stony look and a crisp, 'We'll discuss it later,' after which he'd promptly returned to his endless phone calls.

That he was returning to Palermo had become clear during a particularly heated conversation.

Her heart flipped over hard at the thought of him returning to the place that had given him such a rough start in life.

He looked up then, and their eyes connected. For a moment, she thought she saw a flare of pain mingled with hope. But his expression hardened and his gaze veered away. This time, her heart bypassed the somersault stage and went straight for cracking right down the middle.

She was still trying to hold herself together when he took a break to eat and play with Lucca. He stopped by her armchair on the way back to where he'd set up his office and looked down at her.

'I have a team childproofing my London apartment and another scouting for a place in Dublin. Emily will be flying out to help take care of Lucca when he's with me. Is that acceptable to you?'

As she stared up at his grim face, her heart broke all over

again. Slowly, she nodded. 'I won't keep him away from you. I just need a reasonable heads-up when you're coming to see him, so I can arrange it with the playgroup.'

His mouth compressed and he nodded. '*Bene*, it will be done.' He walked away to the far side of the plane and didn't speak to her again until they landed.

As predicted, Lucca turned hysterical at the idea of his father leaving. Maisie watched, a stone lodged in her throat, as Romeo hugged him on the tarmac and reassured him that his absence wouldn't be a long one. After several minutes, Lucca calmed down and Romeo strode to where she stood.

He handed Lucca over, his hand lingering on his son before his jaw clenched. 'I'll be in touch in the next few days, a week at the most, to arrange a time to see him. And I'll call him tonight.'

'Um…sure.'

With another look at his son, Romeo turned and walked back into his plane.

Maisie stood frozen, her mind reeling at the thought that her marriage was ending right then and there, on a painfully bright summer's day in Dublin.

She clutched Lucca closer as he whimpered at his departing father. Romeo disappeared, and Lucca began to weep.

Forcing herself to move, she strapped him into his seat in the sleek car waiting for them, then buckled herself in next to him.

The sun was still shining when they pulled up outside her restaurant despite it being evening. Unable to face going in, she waved at a gawping Lacey and went straight up to her apartment. Her heart sank when a knock came at the door less than an hour later.

She opened it to Bronagh, who was trying hard to pretend she wasn't shocked to see her.

'I've just put Lucca down for the night. Do you want to come in for a cup of tea?' Maisie offered.

'Tea is great, but *you* look like you need something stronger.' Bronagh held out a bottle of red wine, the concern she was trying to hide finally breaking through.

By her third glass, Maisie had broken down and spilled every last pathetically needy feeling.

'So…what are you going to do?' Bronagh asked when Maisie stopped to toss back another fortifying gulp of wine.

Maisie looked up. 'Oh, please don't worry that I'm going to take over again at the restaurant. To be honest, I could do with the break.'

Bronagh shook her head. 'That wasn't what I meant. What are you going to do about Romeo?'

Maisie frowned. 'What do you mean? It's over.'

'You really think so? From what you said he didn't *have* to marry you. This is the twenty-first century and he's rich enough to afford a dozen armies to protect you and Lucca if he wanted to without putting a ring on your finger.' She nodded to Maisie's hand. 'And you're still wearing your wedding rings. Is he still wearing his?'

Maisie nodded abstractedly and frowned at the sparkling rings. 'What are you saying?'

Bronagh shrugged. 'That things seem awfully *unresolved* for two people hell-bent on chucking in the towel so quickly.'

'I'm not…I wasn't… He only wants sex.' She blushed and drank some more wine.

'Of course he does. Sex is the easiest way to hide deeper emotion, that's why it's called angry sex, rebound sex, make-up sex…need I go on?'

Miserably, Maisie shook her head.

Bronagh laid a gentle hand on her arm. 'You haven't known a lot of love in your life, but then neither has he. One of you has to be brave enough to scratch beneath the surface.'

'Why do I have to do the scratching?' Maisie blurted. 'Just because he thinks I'm a wildcat in bed doesn't mean… *God!* I can't believe I just said that.'

Bronagh laughed and rose. 'I think the jet lag and wine are doing their job. Get some sleep. I'll take the monitor with me when I go downstairs in case Lucca wakes up.'

Maisie hugged her friend, her thoughts rioting as she prepared for bed. When she lay wide awake three hours later, she wasn't surprised.

Bronagh's words raced through her mind.

While she didn't think she'd misinterpreted her conversations with Romeo, was it possible she'd blinded herself to a different possibility?

Could she guide Romeo into loving her? He might have been devoid of love before he'd arrived on her doorstep three weeks ago, but Maisie had seen what he felt for his son. And Romeo hadn't rejected the love that poured from Lucca. Surely he couldn't rule it out of his life for ever?

Turning over, she exhaled slowly, careful not to let too much hope take root.

When Romeo arrived on Saturday, she would try to broach the subject, see if there was a glimmer of anything worth pursuing.

Except Romeo didn't come on Saturday. He sent Emily and a team of bodyguards after calling with his apologies. He'd established a routine with Lucca where they video-called for half an hour in the morning and half an hour in the evening. His greetings to Maisie when she connected his calls were cool and courteous. Any attempt at a conversation was quickly curbed with a demand for his son.

By the time he cancelled on Saturday, she knew, once again, she'd been foolish to hope. Yet she couldn't bring herself to take off her wedding rings. Nor could she find the strength to tell Lucca that, no, Mummy and Daddy would never live together again.

Admitting to herself that she was burying her head in the sand didn't stop her from doing exactly that. She helped out in the restaurant when she could, but even there she knew she wasn't on her full game, so she kept her presence to a minimum.

And then Romeo stopped calling.

For the first two days, she didn't have time to worry because she had her hands full controlling Lucca's misery-fuelled tantrums.

By the third day she was debating whether to call him. She talked herself out of it for half a day before dialling his number. It went straight to voicemail. Leaving a garbled message guaranteed to make her sound like a lunatic, she sat back, her stomach churning.

When he hadn't called by evening, she marched downstairs and strode across the road to where one of his guards was stationed.

'Have you heard from your boss?'

The thickset man frowned. 'My boss is across the road.' He indicated another heavily muscled man wearing wrap-around shades.

She sighed, exasperated. 'I mean your boss's boss. Mr Brunetti.'

'Oh. Sorry, miss, I don't have his number.'

'It's not miss, it's Mrs...Brunetti.' She waved her rings, unnecessarily, then cringed inside. 'I need to speak to Mr Brunetti.'

The man snapped to attention, then quickly strode over to his boss. The hushed conversation ensued and Wraparound Shades approached.

'I'm sorry, Mrs Brunetti, but Mr Brunetti requested that his whereabouts not be disclosed.'

Panic flared through her belly. 'Why?'

A shrug. 'He didn't say. I'm sorry.'

Maisie raced back upstairs, her heart crashing wildly against her ribs. She tried Emily's number and got a message to say she was on sabbatical in Hawaii.

She spent the night pacing her living room, alternating

between leaving a message and hitting Romeo's video-call button. Both went unanswered.

By mid-morning she was frantic. And angry. And miserable. For herself and for her son. But mostly, she was angry with Romeo.

Yanking her front door open, she faced the head bodyguard, arms folded. 'I'm about to buy a round-the-world plane ticket and drag my four-year-old to go and look for his missing father. I'm assuming your job includes accompanying us on trips abroad?'

He nodded warily.

'Good, then consider this your heads-up. We're leaving in an hour. I intend on starting in…oh, I don't know… Outer Mongolia?'

His eyes widened.

'Or perhaps you can save us all a wasted journey and tell me what country I should start in.'

The man swallowed, shifted from foot to foot. Maisie glared harder. 'You should start in Italy.'

The relief she'd expected never materialised. If Romeo was in Italy, then… 'Specifically in Palermo?'

Another wary nod.

She raced back to her flat and opened her laptop. The restaurant was closed today, and Bronagh had issued a standing babysitting assistance.

After debating whether to take Lucca with her, she decided against it, called Bronagh to tell her to pick up Lucca from nursery and booked a solo ticket.

Until she knew where Romeo was and the reason for his silence, she wasn't risking taking their son to Palermo.

After flying in Romeo's private jet, her cramped economy seat felt like torture. She emerged from the flight hot, sweaty and filled with even more panic when she realised she had no idea where to start looking for Romeo.

The last time she'd done this she hadn't been in possession of a last name.

This time the last name was one that held such power and prestige that, in her state of dishevelled hair and worn jeans, she would probably achieve the same results as last time. Laughter and ridicule.

Hailing a taxi to a three-star hotel, she quickly texted Bronagh to say she'd arrived, then showered, changed into a blue cotton dress and clipped her hair at her nape. Smoothing on lip gloss, she froze for a second when she realised it was the same dress she'd worn the night she'd met Romeo.

Hand shaking, she capped the tube and grabbed her bag.

The weather was much hotter in July than it had been the last time she was here, and a sheen of sweat covered her arms by the time she made it to Giuseppe's.

Heart thumping, she sat at a table and ordered a *limoncello*. Sipping the cool drink more for something to do than anything else, she tried to think through what she'd say to the only person who could give her answers as to Romeo's whereabouts—Lorenzo Carmine.

Whether the old man would actually answer her questions was a bridge she'd cross when she came to it. According to the article she'd found online, Lorenzo lived in a mansion once belonging to Agostino Fattore, a man whose picture bore a strong resemblance to Romeo, once you dragged your gaze from the skin-crawling cruelty in his eyes.

Her fingers curled around her glass, her stomach churning in horror at what the man she loved had suffered. Was probably still suffering…

Shutting her eyes, she dropped her head into her hands and breathed in deep. She wouldn't think the worst. She would get her chance to tell Romeo exactly how she felt.

All of it. With nothing held back.

Firming her jaw, she opened her eyes and jerked upright in shock.

He was pulling back the chair at the adjacent table. Sunglasses obscured his eyes and the direction of his gaze suggested he wasn't looking at her, but Maisie knew Romeo had seen her.

Her body's sizzling awareness was too strong to be anything but a reaction to his direct scrutiny.

A judder shook its way up from her toes as she stared at him, relief pounding through her to see him in one piece. Hungrily her eyes roved over him. His cheekbones looked a little more prominent, and his mouth a lot grimmer, but there was no mistaking the powerful aura emanating from him or his masculine grace when he curled elegant fingers around the tiny espresso cup the waiter slid onto his table a few minutes later.

He picked up the beverage, knocked it back in one greedy gulp, then stood, extracted a ten-euro note from his pocket and placed it on the table.

She sat poised in her chair unable to believe he would just leave without speaking to her.

Then his arrogant head turned her way. Heat sizzled over her skin, far hotter than the sun's rays as she stared back at him. His hands clenched into fists, then released.

Without a word, he strode onto the pavement leading away from the waterfront.

Maisie grabbed her handbag and raced after him. Everything about his quick strides and tense shoulders suggested he didn't want to be disturbed. But she hadn't come all this way to be turned away.

He turned into a vaguely familiar street five minutes later. When she recognised it, she froze, her pulse tripling its beat as she read the name of the hotel.

She jerked into motion when Romeo disappeared inside. By the time she entered the jaw-dropping interior of the marble-floored atrium, he was gone. She bit her lip and looked around the plush surroundings, wondering whether she would receive the same humiliating reception as she had last time.

'Signora Brunetti!' A sharply dressed man hurried towards her, his hand proffered in greeting.

'Um, yes?'

'I was asked this morning to look out for you and inform you that the room you seek is Penthouse One.'

'Ah…thank you.'

'*Prego.* If you'll come with me, I'll personally access the private lift for you.'

He escorted her to the lift, inserted the key and pressed the button, before stepping back with a respectful bow.

Clutching her bag against her chest, Maisie willed her pulse to stop racing. But it was no use. Now that she'd seen that Romeo was unharmed, every ounce of adrenaline was churning towards the emotional undertaking she was about to perform.

Should that fail…

Her knees buckled and she sagged against the gilt-edged mirrored walls as the lift doors opened. Sucking in a deep breath, she forced one foot in front of the other. The pristine white doors and gold-encrusted knobs loomed large and imposing in front of her.

Lifting a hand, she knocked.

CHAPTER FIFTEEN

HE OPENED THE DOOR after the third round of knocking. And said nothing. Bleak hazel eyes drilled into hers, seething emotions vibrating in the thick silence.

Maisie cleared her throat.

'You haven't called in four d-days. Our son is miserable without you,' she stammered when she eventually found her brain.

Romeo's face twisted with agonised bitterness and regret, before it resettled into stark blankness. 'I'll make it up to him. My business in Palermo took longer than I thought. I have a month-long business commitment in London starting next week. Once I'm settled, Emily will resume coordinating with you on visiting schedules. I'll also have my team provide you with useful numbers including my pilot's so you don't have to rely on commercial travel. There's a car waiting for you downstairs right now. My plane will take you back home. Have a safe trip back. *Arrivederci.*'

He shut the door in her face.

Her mouth dropped open in shock for several seconds before, temper flaring, she slapped her open palm repeatedly on the door. When he yanked it open, his face was a mask that covered a multitude of emotions. Emotions he was hell-bent on keeping from her.

'I came all this way and that's all you have to say to me?'

He shoved his hands deep into his pockets. 'What more is there to say? You've made it more than clear our son is the only subject on the table when it comes to you and me.'

'That's not true,' she replied.

His jaw worked. 'Dammit, what the hell do you want from me, Maisie?' he demanded gutturally.

'For starters, why did you tell the concierge my name with the instructions to let me up when I arrived?'

'Because you're the mother of my child, and still my wife—at least until one of us decides to do something about it. And also because I have security watching over you and Lucca twenty-four hours a day. I was told the moment you bought a plane ticket to Sicily. I thought I'd save you the trouble of an awkward enquiry at the front desk when you eventually got here.' The thinly veiled mockery made her skin sting.

Nervously, she shifted on her feet. 'Well…okay. I'm here. So are you going to let me in?' she asked with a fast-dwindling bravado.

He raised an eyebrow. 'Are you sure you want to come in? Surely this room holds bad memories for you.'

She looked over his shoulder and caught sight of the mixture of opulent and beautiful antique and modern furniture, some of which they'd appreciated up close and personal with their naked bodies. 'They weren't all bad,' she murmured huskily. 'In fact, the night before the morning after was quite spectacular. One of the best nights of my life.'

He froze, his hazel eyes flaring a bright gold before a cloud descended on his face. 'What a shame it is then that your worst was finding yourself married to me.' His voice leaked a gravel roughness coated with pain and her heart squeezed.

'Don't put words in my mouth, Romeo. I said I didn't want to be married to you. I didn't say it was because I hated the idea. Or you.'

Tension filled his body. 'What did you mean?' he asked raggedly.

'Are you going to let me in?'

He jerked backwards, his hand rigid around the door-knob. His warmth seemed to reach out to her as she passed him, his scent filling her starving senses so headily, she almost broke down and plastered herself against him.

The suite was just as she remembered. The luxurious gold-and-cream-striped sofa stood in the same place she'd first made love with Romeo. She dropped her handbag on it, her fingers helplessly trailing over the exquisite design as memories flooded her.

Unable to resist, she touched the glass-topped console table set between two floor-to-ceiling windows, then the entertainment centre, where Romeo had played *Pagliacci's* mournful theme tunes while he'd feasted on her.

'Do you wish me to leave you alone to reminisce?' he enquired tightly.

She turned to find him frozen against the closed door, his arms folded. He wasn't as calm as he appeared, a muscle flicking in his jaw as he watched her.

'Why are you standing over there, Romeo? Are you afraid of me?' she challenged, even though her heart banged hard against her ribs.

A harsh laugh barked from him, then his face seemed to crumple before he sliced his fingers through his hair. '*Sì*, I'm afraid. I'm terrified of what I feel when I'm around you. And even more terrified of my emotions when I'm not.'

The naked vulnerability in that announcement strangled her breath. The room took on a brightness that made her blink hard. Then she realised the brightness was her heart lifting from the gloom, hope rising fast and hard, against her will.

'What are you saying, Romeo?' She couldn't allow room for misinterpretation. The stakes were higher than ever this time.

He exhaled. Deep and long and shakily, his massive chest quaking beneath his black shirt. 'I mean, I love you, Maisie. Of course, I could be mistaken because I really don't know what love is. But I feel a ravaging emptiness every second of every day that I have to survive without you. I thought I knew what it felt to contemplate a hopeless future until the day you told me you regretted marrying me.' He shook his head and surged away from the door.

Striding to the window, he stared down into the street. 'I haven't been able to function since that moment. You're all I think about, all I crave...' Another juddering breath. 'Is that love? This feeling of desperate hopelessness?' he intoned bleakly.

Maisie moved until she was a few feet from him, desperate to touch him. 'I don't know, Romeo. Do you feel the same ache when you imagine us being together instead of apart? Or is it different, better?' she whispered.

His head dropped forward, his forehead resting against the cool glass as a tremble moved through his body. '*Per favore*...please, *gattina*, why are you doing this?' he groaned roughly. 'Why are you here?'

Maisie swallowed. 'I needed to see that you're all right. That Lorenzo—'

'Lorenzo is no longer an issue. The *famiglia* are abandoning his sinking ship. We have a witness who'll testify to what happened to Zaccheo's father after my father threw me out that night. Lorenzo is now facing a murder charge. Our combined testimony will put him away for good.'

She gasped. 'Why did he attack Zaccheo's father?'

'Paolo Giordano had the task of disposing of me after my mother left me on my father's doorstep. My father didn't want me, so Paolo took me home. Unfortunately, his wife was less than enthusiastic about having another mouth to feed. Paolo had the audacity to offend my father by trying to return me to him after a month. My father set Lorenzo on him.' He stopped, distant memories glazing his eyes before he shook them off. 'I made a statement to the chief of police two days ago. He issued warrants for Lorenzo's arrest. The case may collapse or it may not. Either way, Lorenzo is going to spend some time in prison before the case goes to trial. He'll know better than to come after me or mine again.'

'So, that was how you ended up on the streets? Because your mother didn't want you?'

'She was a high-class prostitute. Getting pregnant with me put a huge obstacle in her chosen career. When I became too much for her, she drove me to a house I'd never visited before, told me it was my father's house and drove away.'

'Did you see her again?'

He closed his eyes for a split second. 'Not until I stayed with her for a week, here in Palermo, five years ago.'

'The week we met?'

He nodded. 'She called, finally. After years of silence, she called me. I'd kept tabs on her over the years and knew when she fell on particularly hard times. I found ways to send her money without her knowing it came from me. I didn't want her contacting me because I was rich. I wanted her to do it because I was her son and she wanted to see me.' He shook his head, bitterness and pain warring over his face. 'The week before she died, she finally called. I was elated.'

'What happened?'

'She wanted the use of my credit card. She wasn't interested in who I was or whether I could afford it. She had a fast-growing brain tumour and didn't have long to live. She wanted to die in style. I checked her into the presidential suite at the Four Seasons. And I stayed with her, hoping that she'd show me, in some small way, that she'd regretted giving me away. She didn't. I held her hand until she passed away and all she did was curse me for looking like my father.

'So, you see, I don't know if this living, breathing thing inside me is love, or if it's a twisted need to cling to something that's damaged because I've touched it.'

The words wrenched at her soul. 'Please don't say that.'

He turned to face her, and his eyes were deep dark pools of pain. 'That day we met was the first time I accepted that hope was a useless emotion. That love didn't exist. Not for people like me.'

'Romeo…'

'It's okay, *gattina*. I know you don't love me.' His shoulders drooped in weary, agonised defeat. 'I'll make sure the divorce is fast and the settlement more than generous.'

Her breath shook. 'I don't want a divorce or your money, Romeo.'

A sound of a wounded animal seared from his throat. She took the final step and placed her left hand on his chest. 'If I did, I would've taken off my wedding ring the moment we left Hawaii.'

His gaze fell on her ring and his eyes flared bright, and then dimmed almost immediately. As if a light had gone off inside.

'We can't stay married simply for the sake of Lucca. I won't be responsible for bringing unhappiness to your life.'

'Then bring happiness. Love me. Be with me.'

His eyes slowly rose, connected with hers. 'But on the island, you said—'

'I said I didn't want to be married because I couldn't bear the thought of loving you and not having you love me back.'

His eyes widened and he jerked upright, his strong arms closing on her shoulders. *'Che cosa?'*

Tears brimmed her eyes. 'I love you, Romeo. I've loved you since the night we spent in this room. I've been miserable without you and I really don't want a divorce, if you don't mind,' she pleaded in a wobbly voice.

'I don't mind,' he responded, his face and voice dazed. 'If you let me, I intend to not mind for at least a dozen lifetimes.'

That bright light ripped through her senses once again. This time she embraced it. Revelled in its warmth. 'Good, because that's how long it'll take for me to show you how much you mean to me, too.'

'*Dio mio, gattina...*' His voice held humble worship, a touching vulnerability that made her cup his face.

'Hold me, Romeo. Kiss me. I've missed you so much.'

With a groan, he sealed his lips to hers.

Three hours later, she dragged her head from his chest and the soothing sound of his heartbeat. 'Are you ready to video-call with Lucca?'

Romeo raised his head and kissed her mouth. 'Hmm, I think I've finally come up with something that'll make him forgive me for not being in touch these past few days.'

'Oh, what's that?'

'A promise of a brother or sister.'

Maisie's heart leapt. She planted a kiss of her own on his willing lips. 'I think you just elevated yourself to *Best Father Ever* status.'

Romeo laughed and set up his laptop after Maisie alerted Bronagh to the incoming call.

Seconds later, the screen filled with their son's beautiful face. 'Mummy! Daddy, when are you coming home?' he demanded plaintively.

Romeo exchanged glances with her. 'We will be there by the time you wake up tomorrow, *bel raggazo.*'

'Okay! I've been learning some Itayan words, Daddy.' He gazed keenly into the screen.

Romeo's hand found hers, and he pressed it to his chest. 'Tell me,' he invited softly.

'*Ti amo, Papà,*' he said haltingly, then his face widened in a proud smile. 'It means, I love you, Daddy.'

Beneath her hand, Romeo's heart lurched, then raced wildly. His throat worked for several moments, before he spoke. 'That is exactly right, and I...' His eyes connected with hers, and tears brimming in hers, she nodded in encouragement. 'I love you, too.'

They rang off several minutes later, and Romeo took her in his arms and just held her. Somewhere in the suite, a mournful opera started.

'Why do you listen to those things? They're so sad.'

He hugged her closer. 'It was a reminder that hope was a futile emotion, that everything dies in the end. But now it'll be a reminder that even in the bleakest moments, the voices of heaven can still be heard.'

She raised her head and stared deep into his soul, her heart turning over. 'I love you, Romeo.'

He kissed her, accepting her love.

He hadn't said he loved her after that first time. But she didn't mind, because she felt it in every touch, every look, and knew he would get around to saying it again eventually, when their world grew less shaky with the depth of emotion rocking them.

When he raised his head, his eyes shone with a brightness that seared her with happiness, right to her very fingertips.

'I see you got away with not being taken to task by Lucca.'

He laughed. 'But I still intend to keep my promise to him and provide him with a brother or sister. Soon,' he stated with serious intent.

She traced his mouth with her fingers. 'Soon. I can think of nothing I want more than another baby with you.'

He gently turned her around and caressed her belly with both hands. Then his strong arms slid around her, swaying her to the sound of angels' voices.

'You're my beginning and my end, *il mio cuore*. My everything.'

EPILOGUE

Three years later

'WHO CAME UP with the brilliant idea that it'd be fun to pack seven hyperactive kids and two overachieving fathers onto a yacht for a vacation?' Eva grumbled as she chased after her ten-month-old daughter crawling at top speed towards the boat's chrome railing. Baby Donatella Giordano immediately screeched in protest at her thwarted bid for freedom.

Maisie grinned, raising her face to the dazzling Mediterranean sunshine. 'You think there would've been any stopping Romeo or Zaccheo once they co-bought the super-yacht they'd been drooling over for a year?'

Eva walked across the wide marble-tiled second-floor deck of the stunning vessel to join Maisie, her white bikini accentuating her tanned skin beautifully. Sitting down, she bounced Donatella on her lap until she quieted. 'It's a beautiful boat, but I haven't been able to sleep a wink from worrying that one of the boys will throw themselves overboard just for the sheer hell of it.'

'Romeo assures me that's impossible. Trust me, I grilled him for hours on that very subject before I agreed to bring Lucca and Marcelo.'

Two-year-old Marcelo glanced up at the mention of his name and grinned from where he splashed in the shallow pool with the second set of Giordano twins, Gianni and Angelo.

Eva kissed the top of her baby's head and sighed happily.

'It's good to see them relax, though, isn't it? I just wish they wouldn't relax so...*vigorously.*'

Maisie laughed and glanced to the side as two power-ful Jet Skis whizzed by, trailed by excited cheers and urges to *go faster.*

Romeo's jet carried Lucca and Zaccheo's his oldest sons.

As they made a final turn past the boat, Romeo's gaze met hers. The contact was brief, but the love blazing in his eyes snagged Maisie's breath. Her heart raced as the over-whelming love, which incredibly grew stronger every day, pounded through her blood. She reached up and touched lips that still tingled from when they'd made love hours ago. Then her hand drifted down to her flat belly, and the surprise that would bring another smile of joy to her hus-band's face.

'Since Romeo hasn't crowed about it, I'm guessing he doesn't know yet?' Eva asked, glancing pointedly at Maisie's stomach.

Maisie gasped. 'No, he doesn't, but how...?'

'Please. You've been positively glowing since you stepped aboard the *Dolcezza Gattina* yesterday. I'm guess-ing you didn't get a chance to tell him because Zaccheo mo-nopolised his attention until the early hours?'

Maisie snorted. 'He didn't come to bed until five this morning.' Whereupon he'd woken her and made love to her until she'd been too exhausted to move. By the time she'd woken again, he'd been up with their children. 'I'll tell him tonight.'

'Tell me what, *amore mio*?'

Maisie jumped guiltily at the deep voice that heralded her husband's arrival.

Romeo climbed the last step and headed straight for her. This close, his tight, lean physique, damp from the ocean's spray, was even more arresting. 'If I told you now, it wouldn't be a surprise, would it?' she finally said when she could speak past the wondrous reality that this gorgeous, incredible man belonged to her.

After kissing his younger son, he lowered his body onto her lounger and braced his hands on either side of her hips, caging her in. Outside the unique cocoon that wrapped itself around them whenever they were this close, Maisie peripherally saw Zaccheo greet his wife with a kiss; heard the staff attend to the children.

But she only had eyes for the man who stared down at her with an intensity that hadn't abated since the first moment they'd set eyes on each other.

'Is there any reason it needs to wait till tonight?' he asked with a thick rasp that spoke of other urgent desires.

She scrambled for a sound reason, but in the end couldn't find one. 'No.'

'Bene.' He stood and held out his hand. 'Come.'

Her excitement ratcheted another notch, but she paused as she stood. 'The children…'

His fingers tightened around hers. 'Emily has everything in hand.'

Romeo led his wife to the master suite and shut the door behind them.

Surprise or not, he would've found a way to bring her here at the first opportunity. Because he couldn't get enough of her. Of her love, her devotion to him, to their family. Of everything.

He pulled her bikini-clad body close now and exhaled with happiness when her arms slid around his neck.

'I love you.' She sighed against him.

He shuddered hard, those three words never ceasing to move him. *'Ti amo anch'io,'* he replied gruffly. 'I'm so thankful you made that journey to Palermo three years ago.'

'So am I, but I'd like to think you would've found your way to me sooner or later. You just needed to put your ghosts to rest.'

He nodded. The ghosts *had* finally been slain. Lorenzo Carmine had been found guilty of murder and jailed, never to breathe free air again. The rest of the *famiglia* had scattered to the wind, bringing an end to Agostino Fattore's poisoned legacy.

Romeo had resisted the urge to raze the Fattore mansion to the ground, instead renovating it with Maisie's help and donating it to the local orphanage.

From the trauma of his childhood and the bleak landscape he'd anticipated his future being, he was now submerged in love and happiness so profound, it scared him sometimes. Not enough that he would fail to hang on to it with both hands.

He pulled his wife closer. 'So, about my surprise?' he pressed as he tugged at the strings of her bikini.

Breathtaking blue eyes met his as she captured his hand, kissed his palm, then laid it gently over her stomach.

His heart stopped, then raced with pure bliss. 'Another baby?' he murmured in awe.

Maisie nodded, tears filling her eyes.

Dropping to his knees, he kissed her belly, and the miracle nestled within. *'Ciao, bella bambina,'* he whispered.

She smiled. 'You're so sure it's a girl this time?'

'I'm certain. She'll be as beautiful as her mother. And she will go a little way to balancing out the testosterone you find so challenging.'

She laughed as he scooped her up and tumbled her into bed.

Laughter ceased, and desire took over. They expressed their love in the gentle kisses and furnace-hot lovemaking.

A few hours later, they dressed and joined their children and the Giordanos around the large dinner table.

Their news was greeted with hugs and kisses, after which Zaccheo raised his glass.

'To family,' he toasted, glancing at every face around the table until finally resting lovingly on his wife. 'And to love.'

'*Sì*, to family,' Romeo echoed. Then his gaze found Maisie's. 'To my for ever,' he murmured for her ears alone.

* * * * *

You can read Zaccheo's story in
A MARRIAGE FIT FOR A SINNER
Available now!

MILLS & BOON®
Hardback – December 2015

ROMANCE

The Price of His Redemption	Carol Marinelli
Back in the Brazilian's Bed	Susan Stephens
The Innocent's Sinful Craving	Sara Craven
Brunetti's Secret Son	Maya Blake
Talos Claims His Virgin	Michelle Smart
Destined for the Desert King	Kate Walker
Ravensdale's Defiant Captive	Melanie Milburne
Caught in His Gilded World	Lucy Ellis
The Best Man & The Wedding Planner	Teresa Carpenter
Proposal at the Winter Ball	Jessica Gilmore
Bodyguard...to Bridegroom?	Nikki Logan
Christmas Kisses with Her Boss	Nina Milne
Playboy Doc's Mistletoe Kiss	Tina Beckett
Her Doctor's Christmas Proposal	Louisa George
From Christmas to Forever?	Marion Lennox
A Mummy to Make Christmas	Susanne Hampton
Miracle Under the Mistletoe	Jennifer Taylor
His Christmas Bride-to-Be	Abigail Gordon
Lone Star Holiday Proposal	Yvonne Lindsay
A Baby for the Boss	Maureen Child

MILLS & BOON®
Large Print – December 2015

ROMANCE

The Greek Demands His Heir	Lynne Graham
The Sinner's Marriage Redemption	Annie West
His Sicilian Cinderella	Carol Marinelli
Captivated by the Greek	Julia James
The Perfect Cazorla Wife	Michelle Smart
Claimed for His Duty	Tara Pammi
The Marakaios Baby	Kate Hewitt
Return of the Italian Tycoon	Jennifer Faye
His Unforgettable Fiancée	Teresa Carpenter
Hired by the Brooding Billionaire	Kandy Shepherd
A Will, a Wish...a Proposal	Jessica Gilmore

HISTORICAL

Griffin Stone: Duke of Decadence	Carole Mortimer
Rake Most Likely to Thrill	Bronwyn Scott
Under a Desert Moon	Laura Martin
The Bootlegger's Daughter	Lauri Robinson
The Captain's Frozen Dream	Georgie Lee

MEDICAL

Midwife...to Mum!	Sue MacKay
His Best Friend's Baby	Susan Carlisle
Italian Surgeon to the Stars	Melanie Milburne
Her Greek Doctor's Proposal	Robin Gianna
New York Doc to Blushing Bride	Janice Lynn
Still Married to Her Ex!	Lucy Clark

MILLS & BOON
Hardback – January 2016

ROMANCE

The Queen's New Year Secret	Maisey Yates
Wearing the De Angelis Ring	Cathy Williams
The Cost of the Forbidden	Carol Marinelli
Mistress of His Revenge	Chantelle Shaw
Theseus Discovers His Heir	Michelle Smart
The Marriage He Must Keep	Dani Collins
Awakening the Ravensdale Heiress	Melanie Milburne
New Year at the Boss's Bidding	Rachael Thomas
His Princess of Convenience	Rebecca Winters
Holiday with the Millionaire	Scarlet Wilson
The Husband She'd Never Met	Barbara Hannay
Unlocking Her Boss's Heart	Christy McKellen
A Daddy for Baby Zoe?	Fiona Lowe
A Love Against All Odds	Emily Forbes
Her Playboy's Proposal	Kate Hardy
One Night...with Her Boss	Annie O'Neil
A Mother for His Adopted Son	Lynne Marshall
A Kiss to Change Her Life	Karin Baine
Twin Heirs to His Throne	Olivia Gates
A Baby for the Boss	Maureen Child

MILLS & BOON®
Large Print – January 2016

ROMANCE

The Greek Commands His Mistress	Lynne Graham
A Pawn in the Playboy's Game	Cathy Williams
Bound to the Warrior King	Maisey Yates
Her Nine Month Confession	Kim Lawrence
Traded to the Desert Sheikh	Caitlin Crews
A Bride Worth Millions	Chantelle Shaw
Vows of Revenge	Dani Collins
Reunited by a Baby Secret	Michelle Douglas
A Wedding for the Greek Tycoon	Rebecca Winters
Beauty & Her Billionaire Boss	Barbara Wallace
Newborn on Her Doorstep	Ellie Darkins

HISTORICAL

Marriage Made in Shame	Sophia James
Tarnished, Tempted and Tamed	Mary Brendan
Forbidden to the Duke	Liz Tyner
The Rebel Daughter	Lauri Robinson
Her Enemy Highlander	Nicole Locke

MEDICAL

Unlocking Her Surgeon's Heart	Fiona Lowe
Her Playboy's Secret	Tina Beckett
The Doctor She Left Behind	Scarlet Wilson
Taming Her Navy Doc	Amy Ruttan
A Promise...to a Proposal?	Kate Hardy
Her Family for Keeps	Molly Evans

MILLS & BOON®

Why shop at millsandboon.co.uk?

Each year, thousands of romance readers find their perfect read at millsandboon.co.uk. That's because we're passionate about bringing you the very best romantic fiction. Here are some of the advantages of shopping at www.millsandboon.co.uk:

* **Get new books first**—you'll be able to buy your favourite books one month before they hit the shops

* **Get exclusive discounts**—you'll also be able to buy our specially created monthly collections, with up to 50% off the RRP

* **Find your favourite authors**—latest news, interviews and new releases for all your favourite authors and series on our website, plus ideas for what to try next

* **Join in**—once you've bought your favourite books, don't forget to register with us to rate, review and join in the discussions

Visit **www.millsandboon.co.uk**
for all this and more today!